JAPANESE DREAMS

JAPANESE DREAMS

FANTASIES, FICTIONS & FAIRYTALES

edited by SEAN WALLACE

LETHE PRESS
MAPLE SHADE, NJ

This trade paperback edition published by
Lethe Press,
118 Heritage Ave,
Maple Shade, NJ 08052.
lethepressbooks.com   lethepress@aol.com

Cover by Steven Segal
Book design by Toby Johnson

ISBN 1-59021-224-X / 978-1-59021-224-0

Library of Congress Cataloging-in-Publication Data

Japanese dreams : fantasies, fictions & fairytales / edited by Sean Wallace.
p. cm.
ISBN-10: 1-59021-224-X (alk. paper)
ISBN-13: 978-1-59021-224-0
1. Fantasy fiction, American. 2. Japan--Fiction. 3. Short stories, American--21st century. I. Wallace, Sean.
PS648.J29J37 2009
813'.0108952--dc22

2009030251

JAPANESE DREAMS

Table of Contents

Introduction

Japan is not a single place. It is at least four: Japan as itself, as it truly is, stripped of all artifice and all lenses through which it is seen. This place is no longer accessible by public transportation—sorry, folks. There is Japan as it sees itself, the mythologies created to explain its history, the elaborate and impenetrable social structures, the divine and immutable hierarchies. Then there is Japan as it is seen by the rest of Asia, often a conqueror, an outlier, an outsider, unique in its relationship with the non-Asian world.

And there is Japan as a dream of the West. A lurid fever-dream, a sensationalistic mash-up of technology and sexuality, a performance enacted for the winners of a war.

I lived in Japan for a little over two years—I went to it as untouched as one may be in the current cultural climate of America, in which the hatred and fear of the Japanese economy of the 1980s has been replaced by a mania for all the many and fascinating products of the same. I did not watch anime, I did not obsess over the history of the Pacific War, I did not long to dress up like a geisha. I knew little about it at all except that I was going there, vaguely uneasy about stepping off of a plane with my imperialistic Navy husband, about what it meant to be an American woman in that country, to stand with so many sailors on Japanese soil.

And so I did what I could do: before I went, I read as many stories as I could. Not tourist guides, not travelogues. Folktales. Fairy tales. I thought that if I could understand them the way I understood Greek myth or the Brothers Grimm, then there could be a kind of home for me there in the terraced hills and pale train stations. There could be a grace, a shared language, a currency between the soul of Japan and the soul of myself. I could say: I bring to you the story of a young writer facing a country of total strangeness, and falling in love with it. I bring to you the story of a young woman not yet ready to be a wife. I bring to you the story of a California girl. And it would give me all these foxes and snow-women and dresses made out of moonlight, samurai hidden inside a peach and eight-headed dragons.

Perhaps this seems silly, naïve. Perhaps it is a child's magical thinking. But you cannot know a place until you know the stories it tells about itself. When you meet a person for the first time, you ask their name, their occupation, how many brothers and sisters they have, what their favorite things to eat are, if they enjoy movies, if they are married. To learn a nation's stories is to enact this same process, to ask it: why are there seasons, where you are from? What does a dog say? Why does the moon change shape? How was the world born? Why must humans die?

If we have more modern ways of answering these questions, that does not mean that the old ways of knowing are not present, in every fox-statue and stick of incense at the base of an obsidian grave. And if you do not know those first things a people answered, you cannot really know anything.

For two years, I listened to stories. I read them in books and on subway walls that pictured tanuki alongside salarymen, I asked housewives to teach me to pray. I learned how to give service to the dead. I marked the calendar in a new way, and set out sacrifices of corn and rice and coins in the shrine below my house. I sat with old women in hot springs while they asked me in halting English if I had found my face in the Fushimi-Inari temple, where there are 33,000 statues of Inari, the Kami of Swordsmiths, Rice, Writers, and Small, Mischievous Animals (surely these last two are redundant), for all the legends say that if you look hard enough, you may find your own face among the thousands of foxes.

To know those things meant worlds more than knowing how to get to Tokyo in less than ninety minutes.

This book can never be a portrait of Japan. There are no Japanese writers in it, for one thing. You shouldn't be surprised. The title gave the game away, really. This is a book of dreams. These are the things we have dreamed of Japan, the radiant hybrids of Japanese myth and Western experience. The beautiful *gaijin* tales of English-speaking writers reaching out their hands towards a country that was born when a jeweled spear pierced the sea, letting fall eight sparkling drops of water when it rose again. These are 33,000 faces of the trickster-god, turning and turning, so that every bristle of fur can be seen, but never all at once. This is the book you must read if you would travel to the secret lands that are half-siblings to the real world, the lands travelers keep in their memories, half-fact, half-dream. This is the Japan of the mind. Its entry fee is so very little, and its treasures vast.

I hope you find your face here.

Catherynne Valente

And the Bones Would Keep Speaking

K. Bird Lincoln

Clouds float into my piece of sky. They are gray and shifting. One almost looks like a fighter plane. Even if the Japanese fighter pilots flew this far inland, they are no connection to my family or the Kiyokawas or the Ugajins, or to any family in Hood River.

Mr. Feldstar made the announcement yesterday morning in math class about Pearl Harbor. I was angry, like everyone else. During the emergency assembly in the gym I took my usual place in the back of the boys' section. I remember the smell of sweat and old socks. I saw Missy and Kara giving me sidelong glances from the girls' section. Then I was ashamed.

I can't imagine living anywhere else than the farm. The New Year's cards that come from Tochigi could be from outer space. I feel closer to the grass I am laying on than to blood-cousins I have never met.

The fighter plane cloud drifts away. I can no longer feel my toes. The bones in my legs ache. I sink into the grass, as if the soil were helping the *hakujin* boys from field worker row by covering their crime.

My head doesn't hurt anymore. I still feel a sticky trickle down the side of my face, but I am pretty sure the bleeding has stopped. I am dying. When I say that to myself it sounds obviously false, like one of Uncle Nobuo's tall tales from Japan.

The sky is bright and blue like it never is in rainy September, and the tops of Otoo-san's apple trees are moving in a wind I can't feel or hear. It is quiet now. Bobby Kent and all the HAKUJIN boys ran away into the silent sunshine. I hate them. I hate every one of them with a ferocity I discover for the first time today. I hate them for the rocks and the pain and the blood. I hate them for making me feel alien and freakish on my own father's land.

I wish I could run away and disappear, too.

My eyes are wide open, my face to the sky. Okaa-san, is that you I'm hearing in the big rocks nearby? Okaa-san, come find me before…

1951

Bella heard the bones on the eve of her first day of high school. The moon was a sliver of light in the dark sky outside her window on the second floor of the old farmhouse. She pushed aside grandma's crazy quilt and went to the window. She knew it was bones, even though it sounded more like a dry rasping than the Halloween rattle of a skeleton.

They newly leveled land spotted with ruts and a few stumps to the west of the house still shocked her. When they first moved here from Michigan, daddy was so excited to finally own his own orchards. Bella wished that the same excited daddy were asleep in the room next to her, instead of the man becoming a stranger to her ever since mama left.

The bones spoke again. She could see nothing but the field outside the window. She would have to go downstairs.

Pulling on a loose sweater, she tiptoed down the stairs, careful to put pressure only on the outside parts of the steps so they wouldn't creak. She flicked on the outside light as she went out the door, then changed her mind and turned it off. Whatever bones were talking outside, they were less scary than dealing with daddy in the dark after one of his binges. It was chilly. Wisps of fog from the river clung to the brush.

It was only eleven-thirty, but the dark was as quiet and thick as the dead of night. Bella followed the bones' rasping down the path that used to cut through the Gravenstein and Macintoshes, ending in a small clearing against Mr. Kiyokawa's strawberry fields on one side and the small strip of forest bordering the bungalows where the field workers lived.

The rasping changed, became more agitated. The sound filled her ears, seeping behind her eyes and forming an ache in her jaw. Her curiosity became irritation. Like she didn't have enough to deal with starting high school tomorrow and daddy still moping around the house waiting for the golf course developers to call, and mama still with her friend in Portland.

Bella didn't notice the figure standing next to a pile of rocks at the edge of the brush until the flare of a match and the steady glow of a cigarette caught her eye.

She stopped, her heart as heavy as a wooden cider press against her lungs. The fog parted, and Bella saw a young man in a leather jacket and hair slicked back with pomade. It was one of the middle Kent boys.

"Little late for you, isn't it?" he said, voice low and husky. He drew deeply on the cigarette and Bella watched ash crumble from the tip into the brown grass.

"I'm starting high school tomorrow," she said. Great. She was such a spaz.

"You're in fat city," he said. Was this Bobby? She couldn't keep them all straight. There were at least five or six of the brothers, all crammed together in one of those tiny cookie cutter houses.

"So what's a chick like you doing out here instead of piling up some z's?" He threw the cigarette on the ground and twisted it under a booted heel.

"I… I thought I heard something," she said. Bobby made a show of looking into the trees and around the field. Then he sat on the largest of the boulders.

"Nothing here but us, doll."

Bella shivered. She was cold. Her heart was still thudding and she couldn't decide if Bobby was making conversation or laughing at her expense. She turned back to the house.

"Holy mother of Jesus!" he said. Bobby leaned down and pulled something long and knotted like a thin tree branch out of the dirt between two of the rocks. "Do you see this?"

Bella stepped close enough to smell pomade and leather. His breath was a bitter white cloud. She looked down at the thing in his hands. It looked like a bone. She reached out to touch it and it made a rasping, sliding noise. Bobby dropped it with a yelp.

"What the… what was that noise?"

Bella started to answer him, but closed her mouth before any words could escape.

1975

Hanako turned the handle to raise the car's window. Her daughter, Kiri-chan, sitting beside her on the worn plastic seat leaned over and pulled her hand away.

"Aren't you hot, mother?" she said. "Let's leave the window open."

Hanako hated that tone of voice. Sometime in the past few years the role of mother and daughter reversed. Now Kiri-chan ordered Hanako's life. It still grated on her. Hanako was a well-used sixty-five, true, but she could still wipe her own ass after using the *benjo,* thank you very much. And she could decide on her own whether to put up a window. The dust from the road was getting in her eyes and making them tear up.

Her son-in-law, the *hakujin*, gave Kiri-chan a look in the rearview mirror. He had kind eyes. Hanako liked him, despite his slightly rancid butter scent and how her grandchildren were doomed to be only half-Japanese. His romantic notions made Hanako worry about the long term, however. The way he held open doors for Kiri-chan, and waited to order at the restaurant near Crater Lake where they stopped for lunch until Kiriko and Hanako ordered first. She hoped he wasn't too soft.

"We're almost there," he said. "Mr. Roberts said he'd meet us at the front gate." Then to Kiri-chan, "I told him we'd only be an hour."

Hanako stared at the seat in front of her. An hour. Just one hour to walk through the field her family had owned, a field full of Hideki's sweat and dreams. One hour to put Mat's ghost to rest. Why had she left this so long?

She should have come back when she was fifty and still spry. But the war, Hideki's arrest, the long months at the interment center in Utah, they were all wounds that never quite healed. Coming back to Hood River would have ripped everything apart.

And now she had just one hour to find her son's bones.

At the turn-off from the highway, Mr. Robertson, the man who bought the farm after they were all sent to the camp at Tule Lake, stood leaning against the gate. He was blonde and sparse, his face lined with something more than just sun and wind. Hanako couldn't resent a face like that.

Wartime was a long time ago, a shameful dream remembered only unwillingly in the thirty years she spent rebuilding their lives in San Francisco. She wondered what her son-in-law told this Robertson. Surely he didn't tell him the truth about her errand. How undignified.

The car rolled to a stop. Hanako allowed Kiri-chan to help her form the car. She presented a furoshiki-wrapped box of red bean-paste cakes to Robertson.

"My thanks for your kindness today," she said. Robertson blushed and averted his eyes when he accepted the package.

Hanako smiled, pleased that Robertson was uncomfortable.

"Okaa-san," said Kiri-chan. "it's getting really hot out here."

Hanako knew what her daughter really meant. Kiri-chan wanted to leave. She thought Hanako was losing her mind. Even the *hakujin,* who had originally been supportive of this trip, was clearing his throat and rolling his eyes when he thought Hanako wasn't looking.

Hanako stooped down, but what she thought might be a finger-bone was only a twig. She threw it away in disgust. Maybe she was crazy. Back in San Francisco she'd had the idea her body would act like a dowsing rod. That somehow, her eldest son's bones would vibrate on a frequency discernible to her own flesh and blood, guiding her steps to where his bones had lain hidden for thirty-five years.

But Hanako felt nothing. She had felt more back at Tule Lake, sitting in the tent watching Ben Kiyohara's breath turn to mist in the cold air. His tale of Mat and the *hakujin* boys from field worker row seemed as insubstantial and fading as the mist. Hanako had tried not to hate Ben for living, or old man Kiyohara for keeping his farm when they lost their own land.

"Konnichiwa," said a clear voice from the gate between the razed field and the Kiyohara land. It was a girl with blonde hair pulled back in a ponytail. She carried a baby with a head of hair like a dark brush on one hip. She came through the gate and carefully shut it behind her. Without hesitation the girl came to stand before Hanako, searching her face in a way that made Hanako blush.

"I'm Bella," said the girl. Hanako's eyes slid from the girl's pale blue, eyes, clear as a ghost's, to the dark brown eyes of her baby. The baby was half. Hanako felt a repulsive fascination as she scanned those features. Would this be her feeling looking at Kiri-chan's baby? She tried to imagine eating a half grandchild's leftover rice such as she did with her grandnieces when they didn't finish their breakfast.

"Konnichiwa," said Hanako.

"My father-in-law, Mr. Kiyohara, told me you were here today," said the girl. The Hakujin came over, hand extended. Bella looked at his hand. The baby gurgled and the girl took the Hakujin's hand in a clumsy grip.

"We won't be bothering Mr. Kiyohara," said the Hakujin. Hanako wished he'd shut up. Like he knew anything. The girl was here to talk to Hanako, she was sure of it.

"I heard…" said the girl, then turned to look at Hanako again with those startling eyes. "When I started high school there was one night I found something strange out here," she said. Hanako wondered at the emotion in her voice. "And then today, Ben and I were visiting from Gresham and Otoo-san told us what you were doing here."

Hanako nodded. Her breath was coming short and quick. This girl knew something about Matsuo. She looked down so the girl would keep talking, but at the same time her ears filled with a white noise like the sound of waves hitting the Oregon coast. The noise grew louder until Hanako could barely make out the girl's words.

"I think I found your son's bones," she said.

The world spun. The field, Kiri-chan, the *Hakujin's* rancid odor, bled together and whirled around the focal point of the girl's finger- pointing towards the boulders at the corner where the old orchard met Kiyohara's orchard, bordered by a strip of forest.

Hanako, half-blind, stumbling, ran to the pile of boulders. She stumbled, fell, and bit her lip as she landed badly on her weak left ankle. Before Kiri-chan could embarrass her, Hanako got up, muscles creaking, and wiped the blood from her mouth. Now she could feel it; a faint vibration emanating from a mid-sized stone at the edge of the pile. Hanako pushed away Kiri-chan's hand and shut her ears to her daughter's stupid cries.

Matsuo? Mat-chan? Imasu ka? Are you there? The blood on her hand stained the rock with streaks of red. As she scrambled in the tall grass beside the rock, Hanako saw what must have happened. She flinched, her skin blackening into bruises as she felt a barrage of blows from words, then fists, and finally rocks.

Her wild American boy, her Mat-chan. She gulped in air, but her lungs felt empty. Of all her children he had belonged the most to the *hakujin* world, and they killed him, beat him to death. She scrabbled in the tough grass. As her hand met the cool weight of bone in the dirt, she heard it.

"Okaa-san? Is that you? Look sharp."

1951

Bobby squatted down, poking through the grass, and came up with another bone.

"Some raccoon must have died here. Creepy," he said. His voice was higher. He sounded nervous and his hand was shaking. Bella could see a streak of pomade staining his collar. His eyes looked wide and innocent in the moonlight. There was a long silence. Their breath mixed and mingled in the chill air.

"I'm shipping out tomorrow," he said, looking up at Bella. "The only way out of this town for me, I guess. Either the army or the jailhouse."

She reached out to wipe the pomade from his collar. Bobby stood up, another slender bone in his hand. Now his eyes narrowed. He let out a ragged breath and turned away for a moment to look through the razed field at Bella's house. When he faced Bella again, the moonlight made his eyes look wet.

The bone rasped again, a rhythm like a song, and Bella understood it's gravelly melody, understood it had come from a boy of the Jap family that used to live here in her house before daddy bought it. The bones sang how white boys from the field worker houses killed the boy. They left him to rot here during the war. Animals had scavenged the bones.

Now Bella's eyes burned. It could just as easily be Bobby's bones here, if he went to Korea. Some girl might stumble on them one night, and mistake them for a raccoon, or whatever they had in Korea. Maybe no one would ever know that Bobby lived or died.

Bella reached for the bone. Bobby, misunderstanding, let it drop and captured her hand in the circle of his chilly fingers instead. He drew her close and buried his nose in her hair. His jacket was softer than it looked- well worn. Bella guessed it was a hand-me-down from his older brothers. They stood there for a moment, their hearts beating together in accompaniment to the singing bones.

"Could I…" Bobby breathed into her hair, "maybe I could write a letter to you from basic training?"

Bella mm-hmmed against his shoulder. There was a marvelous softness moving through her limbs. The bones rasped even louder, more urgently, but she didn't heed their warning. Bella knew it was too late. She would answer Bobby's letters despite everyone's opinion about their ages. She would lie in bed imagining him thinking about her, and this softness would cover her, filling her at night with warmth against her cool sheets.

And then the letters would stop. At a football game where Bella played piccolo in the marching band, the principal would ask for a moment of silence for the local boys who'd fallen. His name would be somewhere near the end, just far down enough that Bella would start hoping. Bella would cry for him all alone, here in the darkness at the edge of her father's razed orchard.

And the bones would keep speaking.

1940

Maybe I am already dead. I can't move. Still, I picture Okaa-san or Otoo-san bursting through the Gravestein trees and finding me. We will get on the bus with the other Japanese farmers going to the Portland Assembly center. Otoo-san will be angry at me for not finishing my chore of nailing the windows shut, but he won't punish me when he sees the blood.

It's no good. The dream blows away like the clouds. They are gone. I was supposed to follow with Ben on his motorcyle after I finished shutting up with house. Maybe he is still waiting for me on the outskirts of town.

Time passes and no one comes. I feel light, as if I might drift off into the sky. Cigarette smoke fills my nostrils. My vision is fragmenting at the edges, only the pale blue sky and the brilliance of the sun are still clear. For a moment, I think I hear a girl's voice. She is crying. Don't be sad. My whole body yearns to touch her. The grass is prickly and bugs, maybe ants, are climbing up my pants leg. My body resonates to the buzz of a cricket, and I can feel the vibration deep in my bones.

Now I am cold. There is only darkness. Okaa-san. Come find me. Look sharp.

ebb and FLOW

EKATERINA SEDIA

I SIT IN MY UNDERWATER PALACE, looking through the window at the schools of bright silent fish drifting in the crystal water, I listen to the sweet music played by jellyfish and seahorses, and I remember. After the love is gone and all the tears are cried out, what else is left to do?

This story does not have a happy ending; they almost never do. The only happy stories you will ever hear are told by men—they spin their lies, trying to convince themselves that they cause no devastation, and that the hearts they break were never worth much to begin with. But I am the one who lives under the sea, keeping it full and salty. I, the daughter of the Sea *kami* Watatsumi. I, who once had a sister and a husband.

I wouldn't have met my husband Hoori no *mikoto* if it weren't for his foolishness. Back on land, he was a ruler of Central Land of Reed Plains, but still he loved to hunt. His brother, Hoderi no *mikoto,* was the best fisherman their young country had ever known. But Hoori was not content with what he had. He talked his brother into trading their jobs for a day.

Hoderi could not use his brother's bow and arrows, and found no game. Hoori was even less successful: not only did he fail to catch any fish, he also lost the fishhook his brother prized above every other possession. Hoderi was upset at the loss, and Hoori swore that he would find it.

He spent days searching the beaches, digging through the mounds of withered kelp, looking under the weightless pieces of driftwood, pale like the moon, turning over every stone, round and polished by the sea into the brightest azure shine. But he didn't find the hook.

He went home and looked at his favorite sword for a long time. It was a katana of the highest craftsmanship, worth more than half of all Japan. Hoori always talked about his weapon with tears in his eyes, as if it were a child or a dear friend. And yet, his love for his brother was stronger than his love for his weapon. He shattered the katana into a thousand pieces, and molded each into a sharp fishing hook, shining in the sun and strong enough to hook a whale.

But Hoderi was not consoled. No matter what Hoori did and how much he pleaded, Hoderi remained firm: he wanted his hook, and no other.

Hoori grew despondent, and spent his days wandering along the shore. The soft susurrus of the waves calmed his troubled heart as they lay themselves by his feet, lapping at his shoes like tame foxes.

He noticed an old man sitting on the beach, throwing pebble after pebble into the pale green waters. Hoori recognized the old man as Shiotsuchi no *kami,* the God of Tides.

"Why are you so sad?" the old *kami* asked.

"I lost my brother's fishhook," Hoori said. "And he would neither talk to me, nor look me in the eye."

Shiotsuchi nodded, and snapped his fingers at the waves. Obedient to his will, they brought him many stems of pliable green bamboo. Fascinated, Hoori watched as the waves reared and spun, shaping the bamboo stems into a giant basket with their watery fingers.

When the bamboo basket was ready, Shiotsuchi helped Hoori into it. "I'll command the tides to carry you to the palace of the Sea God, Watatsumi no *kami*. There is a well by the palace, and a katsura tree growing there. Climb into the tree, and you will be taken to Watatsumi no *kami*. He will be able to help you find the hook, for he is the ruler of all sea creatures."

Hoori thanked the *kami* and settled into the basket. It carried him along with the tides, and the small round waves tossed his bamboo vessel about, playfully but gently.

They carried him all the way to the palace made of fish scales. My home, my life, where my sister and I sang and played under the watchful eye of our father, where all the creatures were our playmates, and even rays would never hurt us but let us ride on their shining backs. Seahorses tangled in our hair, and jellyfish subserviently let us pummel their bells as if they were drums. We dressed in finest silks and sealskin, and never knew a worry in the world.

We didn't know that he was coming.

On that fateful day, you did as you were told. My maid came to the well to fetch me a cup of water—even under the sea we need sweet water to drink. She saw your reflection in the well, and she ran, fearful of strangers, but not before you tore a piece of your jade necklace and dropped it into the cup she carried.

She brought the cup to me, and told me about the stranger in the well. I barely listened as I tilted my cup this way and that, watching the sun play across its golden sides, reflecting from the sparkling jade through the transparent water. It was green and beautiful, and I smiled as the reflected sun dappled my face, warming it. Surely, no evil can come from someone who had a stone like that, I thought.

I called my sister, Tamayoribime, and showed her the stone.

She beamed. "Where did it come from, Toyotamabime?" she asked me.

I told her of what my maid told me, and we went to investigate, our arms twined about each other's waists. We found you in the branches of the katsura tree, the spicy fragrance of its leaves giving you the aura of danger and excitement. You smiled at us and spoke as if you were our equal.

"Come down from that tree," Tamayoribime said.

You did as she told you, although the smile wilted on your face, and your forehead wrinkled in consternation. I guessed that you were not used to being ordered about.

"Please, honored guest," I said. "Come with us so we may introduce you to our father, Watatsumi no *kami*."

You nodded, and looked at me with affection. I lowered my gaze before yours, and you smiled.

We led you through our palace and you grinned in wonderment, tilting your head up to see the cupping roof of the palace, inlaid with mother-of-pearl and decorated with fine drawings done in the octopus ink. You gaped at the tall posts of sandstone and whale ivory holding up the roof, at the twining kelp around them, at the bright lionfish that guarded access to my father's throne room. The guardian let us through, and you stood in astonishment in my father's awesome presence.

He was a great *kami*, and he lay coiled atop of sealskin and silk *tatami*, his skin shining bronze and green, his great bearded head, larger than your entire body, resting on a mound of silk pillows and red and blue jellyfish. A jade incense burner exhaled great clouds of pungent smoke, masking the strong salty smell of my father.

"Come in, Land Prince," my father boomed, his voice shaking the intricate panels of fishbone decorating the walls. "Come in and sit down on my fine *tatami*, and tell me what brings you here."

But you kept silent, your mouth half-open in fascinated attention. My father winked at me, and I called in our entertainers—singing fish, dancing crocodiles, and squid who did magic tricks. Flying fish, tuna and octopus put on a play for you, and two eels played *koto* and *shamisen* by twining their flexible bodies around the instruments' necks and plucking the strings with their tails. You clapped your hands in time with music and laughed like a child. Then your eyes met mine, and you blushed.

My father, who never missed anything that occurred in his palace, sent Tamayoribime and me out with a flick of his tail. He wanted to talk to you *kami* to *mikoto,* I guessed, and obeyed. We left the palace and ran through the forest of kelp, shouting for all the fish to come out and chase us on a pretend hunt. It was dark when we came back, and my father announced that I was to become your wife.

I looked into the marble floor studded with starfish, and did not answer. I never argued with my father; I did not know how.

And so we were married, and I came to love Hoori. I showed him all the secret places my sister and I loved: a grotto of pink stone, with a white sand floor, adored by pearly yellow and blue snails that dotted the walls, gleaming like precious stones; I showed him a large smooth rock where octopi wrote their secret letters in black ink, their tentacles as skillful as the finest brushes; and a dark cave that went down into the bottom of the ocean for miles, gilded with shining algae and populated by phosphorescent moray eels. For our amusement, seahorses staged battles and races, and squid swam in formation, shooting giant ink clouds shaped as flowers to celebrate our love.

Tamayoribime, my sister, rarely joined us on these excursions. Although still young, she understood that the bond the land prince and I shared was not for her to enjoy. She smiled every time she saw me, but I could see the sorrow of her hunched shoulders as she fled to the kelp forest, alone, with only fish for company. My heart ached for her loss, and I wished that gaining a husband did not mean losing my sister. Hoori and I were inseparable, and she grew more distant from me every day, her face close but unreachable, as if it were hidden behind a pane of glass. Hoori had severed the only bond I've ever known, and thus increased my attachment to him; all the love I used to lavish upon my sister was his now.

Days passed, and before we knew it three years had passed since Hoori first entered our palace. I realized that I was pregnant, and told Hoori that he was soon to become a father. He was jubilant at first, but as my belly grew so did the unease in his eyes. He sighed often, and one day I asked what was wrong.

He told me that he missed the land, and was thinking about returning home. "Only," he added, "I still haven't found my brother's fishhook. I cannot go back without it."

"Is this why you came to my father's palace?" I asked.

He bowed his head. "Yes. Only the time here was so delightful that I have forgotten my purpose. Please, Toyotamabime, talk to your father on my behalf."

I obeyed his wishes, as I always did; he was the pearl of my heart, my beloved, so how could I refuse him, even though he wanted nothing more than to return home and leave me behind? I cried as I told my father of Hoori's plea.

His great fins fanned slowly, as he listened to my words. "Well," he said. "I will find that hook for him."

My father's great roar summoned forth all the sea creatures, and Hoori watched with delight as they swam and slithered into the palace, filling it almost to bursting. Fins, tentacles, scales and claws in every imaginable color shimmered and moved everywhere. My father surveyed this living tapestry, and asked everyone in turn whether they've seen the hook.

The fish swore that they haven't, and the crabs and shrimps and scallops promised to sieve through the ocean sand, grain by grain, and to find the hook. Only the sea bream remained silent, although his mouth opened and closed as he strained to speak.

"What's wrong with him?" my father asked the tuna and the ocean perch.

"He hasn't spoken in a while," they said. "Something's been caught in his throat for a long time, and he can neither eat nor speak."

My father extended one of his great but slender claws into the bream's obediently opened wide mouth, and soon it emerged with a shining hook caught in it. The bream breathed a sigh of relief, and apologized for his mistake. But Hoori was so delighted to have recovered his brother's treasure that he paid no mind to the bream's mumbling.

"Thank you, O great Watatsumi no *kami*," Hoori said to my father. "Now I can return home."

I turned away, biting my lip, cradling my bulging belly in my arms. I would not argue, I thought, I would not beg. If the kelp forests and hidden underwater caves were not enough to keep him, what could I do? If the music and singing of the perches and moray eels did not bind him to our palace, what would my feeble voice achieve?

He took my hands, and looked into me eyes. "Toyotamabime, my beloved," he told me. "Will you follow me to the land?"

I'd never been on land before, and the thought filled me with fearful apprehension. Moreover, that would mean breaking away from my father and my sister, from my entire life. But what was I to do? "Let me wait here until it is time for our child to be born," I begged. "Then, build me a parturition hut thatched with cormorant feathers on the beach. I will come there to give birth."

"I'll do as you ask," he said.

"Just promise one thing," I said. "Promise that you will not look into the hut when I am giving birth. Promise me."

His face reflected surprise, but he agreed. "I will send a maid to attend to you," he said.

I shook my head. "My sister will attend to me."

"As you wish," he said, already turning away from me to face my father. "Will you help me get back home?"

"But of course," my father boomed. "One of my fastest *wani* will carry you home. But before you go, please accept this gift from me." With these words, my father produced two jewels, the size of a bream's head, one green, and one pink.

Hoori accepted the gifts with tremulous hands.

My father explained. "The green one is a tide-raising jewel Shiomitsu-Tama, and the other is the tide-lowering jewel Shiohuru-Tama. Use them if you need them."

I smiled at both of them through my tears. In my naiveté, I thought that the jewels were to make our meetings easier, so that Hoori could bring the sea to his doorstep and me with it.

But I was wrong.

When Hoori returned home, born on the back of our swiftest shark, he discovered that Hoderi had a hidden purpose in sending him away to find his hook. (If he had asked me, I would've told him that all that trouble for a fishhook was just silly.) While Hoori was away, Hoderi had taken over the land, installing himself as an Emperor, usurping Hoori's place. I do not know what it is that men usually do to hurt each other; but I do know that Hoori used Shiomitsu-Tama, the jewel of flow, to call the ocean forth and flood his brother's fields, poisoning the land with salt, to steal the breath of Hoderi's men. The ocean flowed onto the land, drowned the fields and people who worked in them, until it rose all the way to the doorstep of Hoderi no *mikoto*'s house.

And we, the inhabitants of the ocean, we suffered too. The ocean fell so low that many of the shallow places were exposed, killing the coral and the slow starfish and sea urchins. Jellyfish flopped on the exposed rocks and collapsed into sad puddles of death. The secret grotto grew too shallow for the snails and they fled, their mantles rustling on the dry sand. That was the price of your triumph.

And when you succeeded in subduing your willful sibling, you lowered the tides, filling back the ocean. Oh, how happy we were that day, and how we mourned those we had lost! But there was little time for mourning; it was time for our child to be born.

Tamayoribime and I dressed in our finest silks, and mounted our loyal whale who took us to the shores of your country. Tamayoribime sang and tried to make conversation, laughing a little desperately, trying to recapture the carefree days of our childhood and failing. Soon, she gave up, leaving me to my thoughts. I worried if you remembered to build the hut, and fretted that you wouldn't be able to resist the temptation to look. And I felt guilty about my deception, about hiding my true nature from you, but when one was born a princess, a daughter of the Sea *kami*, one was bound to have some secrets even one's husband was not meant know.

The night had descended, setting the ocean aflame with many tiny candles lit for us by the tiniest of our subjects, and they reflected in the fine sky canopy of black velvet stretching far above us. The roaring of the waves signaled that the shore was close, and anxiously I searched the outline of the dark beach against the darker sky for the sign of my beloved. I saw a flickering of a lantern mounted on the cormorant-feathered roof of a hut. The hut was small, but warm and dry and richly decorated on the inside. You waited for me there, and the moment our hands met I felt the first pangs of birth pain.

Tamayoribime ushered you outside, into the darkness, where the waves crashed on the shore with a hungry roar and the air tasted of salt spumes. When she returned, she wiped the sweat off my forehead, and comforted me as the contractions grew stronger, and I was no longer able to maintain my human form.

My hair unwound like the seaweed in the current and fell off, and my nose elongated as my mouth jutted forward, pushed wide open by the gleaming triangular teeth. My smooth skin turned into sand and leather, my arms turned into fins, and my legs fused into a muscular tail armored with a crescent fin. As a shark, I writhed in agony of childbirth, my entire body convulsing and my tail whipping the *tatami* covering the earthen floor.

Just as the head of our son, open-eyed and screaming, pushed out of my body and my insides ripped and bled, I heard another scream. With my shark eyes I saw your face, pale against the sky, looking at me through the hole in the roof. Oh, the horror on your face would've been easier to bear than the disgust. Tears rolled from my lidless fish eyes, and with a downward maw, teeth gnashing, I begged and pleaded for your forgiveness, for you to love me again.

The color drained from your face, and I saw that with it all the memories of our life under the ocean drained out of you, as if they never existed. You forgot everything, and could only see the loathsome monster writhing on the ground, between your son and pretty Tamayoribime. What was left for me to do? I fled, lumbering, flopping, awkward, my gills full of sand. I struggled across the beach and into the waiting welcoming arms of the surf. It embraced me, washing away dirt and blood, forgiving, comforting.

I did not look back.

I returned to my father's palace, leaving Tamayoribime to care for my son Ugayafukiaezu. The bond between us had been broken, and even she chose you and the child over me. I could not bear to look at my child or at you, and so I blocked the passage between land and sea, so that the journey between our realms would never again be easy. Only Tamayoribime passed freely, bringing me news of my son's growth, and an occasional poem from you.

I could not bear to hear the singing of fish anymore, and could not forgive them for telling you about the whereabouts of the cursed fishhook, so I took away their voices. Now, they are forever silent, and only the mournful songs of their *koto* and *shamisen* and the silver bells of the jellyfish break the silence of our realm. I listen to their music, so sad, and yet not sadder than my heart. When all the tears are cried out and only memories are left I wander like a ghost in the grand palace made of fish scales, dreaming of the voices of my sister and my husband.

And every time the ocean water churns, I am reminded of the ebb and flow of the tides, of the jewels you still have in your possession. You never use them anymore, not even to bring me closer to you. But every time the water turns toward land, I grow hopeful, and my love for you ebbs and flows with the ocean.

THE GREEN DRAGON

ERZEBET YELLOWBOY

THE DOCKYARD WAS DRY AND cold and smelled of metal. One young man, no more than a shadow among shadows, wound his way silently around scaffolding so high it seemed to reach the clouds in heaven. Kazuo crouched behind a coiled nest of chain as voices echoed through the yard. Sound traveled weirdly among the massive columns and cranes; the men speaking could be anywhere. It would be the end of his career, were the guards to find him. Special permission was required to be in the yard at this time of night; Kazuo had no such permission. The need to obey his commander and all who stood above him in the over-arching hierarchy of family and empire, was strong. His love of Soryu was stronger.

As the youngest of four brothers, Kazuo had always known that his was to be a life of labor. Kazuo never once felt that things should be otherwise and had gladly volunteered his services to the empire by way of the sea, becoming another face among many within the ranks of the Imperial Navy. Kazuo respected the sea—one must feel something for the great water when it dictated the ebb and flow of island life. Some feared it, but Kazuo had not lived enough to know fear.

He was fortunate, he thought as he knelt on the floor, that he hadn't yet been caught. These occasional trysts were all that Kazuo asked of the gods, and he was certain his luck would hold. He was right. The voices faded and he stood, secure in the knowledge that he was, at last, alone with his love. Soon she would leave the dockyard. He might never see her again; though he'd requested it, he had not been assigned to her crew. He could not let her go without saying goodbye.

She rose up before him, her hulking curves gentled by the soft light of several lanterns left glowing in the yard. He dreamed of walking on her decks, of flying a Zero above her as she sliced through the waters of the Pacific, of watching her move over the waves. Kazuo did not long for glory; he simply loved the carrier that rested, for now, at the dockyard where she'd been built.

The air was still, heavy, Kazuo heard movement by his feet. It was a rat, bravely daring the debris strewn about in search of food. Kazuo almost jumped, but he stopped himself, drew a breath. The rat didn't matter. He did not have time to waste on it. These few precious moments were for Soryu alone. He gazed upwards into the night and saw, far above his head, light dancing on the golden chrysanthemum on her prow. He was not a poetic youth, but the flower seemed to be a perfect symbol of all that was beautiful about the warship in front of him. It was this beacon that drew him, time after time, to her side.

Kazuo often wished that Soryu could talk to him. He imagined that it would go something like this:

Kazuo, why do you come to me each night? she always asked.

Because I love you, he always replied.

Instead, it happened like this:

Rather than approach the hull of the ship in his usual manner, Kazuo, distracted by the rat, took an unexpected turn. Suddenly she was there in front of him, with her head bowed and her eyes on his feet as he approached.

"Who are you?" Kazuo whispered to the woman in shock. "Don't you know you aren't supposed to be here?"

And then she raised her head and looked into his eyes. He saw the shape of a flower emblazoned on her forehead, and he knew.

"I am dreaming," he said.

"You are not." The woman spoke, her voice the quiet falling of cherry blossoms onto grass. "I am Soryu, the Green Dragon, and you have called me out from where I was sleeping. Mortal man, what is it that you want of me?"

Kazuo felt his flesh pimple; his hair stood on end. He rubbed his eyes, but the vision was still there. A strange kimono clung to her small form, folding over her body to give the impression of scales. Her hair was arranged neatly about her head; it was the color of the deepest ocean, where no light goes. Her eyes, so like and yet unlike his own, were green and coy, and yet he sensed a sorrow about her that he could not describe, it being yet another thing with which he'd had little experience. He could not doubt that this creature before him was, somehow, his Soryu in human form.

"I want nothing of you but to love you, as I do now." He was not sure how to address someone such as this. He bowed to show his respect; he hoped she understood his gesture.

"Nothing? Nothing at all?" She did not appear to move, yet to Kazuo it seemed that she gave a little flip of her head, a teasing movement designed to entice and confuse him. It worked. What more *could* he want from such as this? Whatever earthly desires he had were nothing when compared to her beauty. He wanted no one and nothing but that which he had declared.

"Only to love you, now and forever," he finally replied.

"Forever is a very long time," she said.

"Yes, it is."

"You are sure of this?" He thought he saw her smile.

"I am sure of it." He was helpless before her, as he had been since he'd first seen her rise up, new, from a design in the minds of men.

"Because you want nothing from me," Soryu said, "I will give you all. Kazuo, you and you alone will have my love." She let her gaze linger on his face, and this time he did see a smile cross her own. And then she was gone, as though she had never been, and Kazuo was alone in the yard again.

Not alone, he thought. Her spirit is here, and she will come back to me, now that she loves me. He stroked the ship's hull before turning away, and walked with reverence back to his bed where he dreamed that he held her until first light.

When next he entered the dockyard, she was gone.

It was no easy time to serve in the Imperial Navy. Victorious battles at sea were tempered by the knowledge that the enemy was capable of out-producing the empire on every level. Details like these, however, were easy to overlook, especially when you were no one in particular, like Kazuo. He had no deep thoughts on the war, not like some of the men, men who had been to the universities and had ideas about liberalism and how the empire could find a place in the new age about to dawn. These things were too grand, too vast for Kazuo. He was content in the knowledge that he loved, and was loved, by Soryu. Nothing else mattered, not even the war itself.

At night, during those few peaceful hours he was allowed to dream of a different life, he often saw himself and Soryu living quietly together in a fisherman's hut, on the shore by the sea, making a small but happy living in each other's care. During the day, when the bright sun beamed down on the docks and his ears were full of the voices of men, calling for more rope or chain, or a hammer or chisel, he had no time to engage in these dreams, but she was always there, beside him. Or so he imagined.

Yet no matter how Kazuo tried to avoid it, war would not avoid him. In Summer word reached the docks—Soryu had been sunk by the enemy. This is the way of war, but all Kazuo could think was that he should have been with her when she went down into the sea. He envied Yanagimoto, the man who stayed with her to the very end, and felt cheated by forces he could not readily name. As he prayed that night, feeling alone for the first time since she had spoken to him, he found a name for those forces. Finally, Kazuo understood that he was at war, and the face of the enemy took shape.

His prayers stopped. He was angry at the gods, at Susano'o and Ryujin, for couldn't they have changed the outcome of that battle? Susano'o and Ryujin were on no man's side, but Kazuo was certain that either of them could have intervened. Either of them could have saved Soryu and returned her safely to Kazuo, who would have done anything for the chance to be with her again. Anything at all.

When the divine wind blew through the empire, Kazuo listened with interest to the rustling it made among the leaves. Men argued quietly among themselves about the need for such a tactic, about the reasons behind the idea and the cost of implementing it. Kazuo listened to the men, but he had no opinions to share. He thought to himself *now, now there is an opportunity for me*. He only had to wait a while longer.

The commander gathered the men together one morning. He described the impending invasion by enemy forces onto the mainland and the dire need for volunteers to hold the enemy at bay. The goal—to dive against the enemy ships and inflict as much damage as possible, for glory of empire, for love of family, for honor of self. The request—to volunteer for the special attack force that was even now paralyzing the enemy at sea. The commander passed out small squares of paper, asked each man to consider his choice. Kazuo did not hesitate. He made his mark—yes, I volunteer.

That night there was even more talk. The men who had volunteered busily packed their bags; they would be shipped out at first light for the training base. Kazuo did not join in the discussions. He sat on his bunk and contemplated his future. It already seemed meaningless without Soryu and he could not attach meaning to his actions now. Not like the others, who believed that they were doing a good thing, or like those who disagreed but had volunteered anyway, because there was no real choice. For Kazuo it was a simple equation. He had been offered a method of confronting the real enemy—the gods who had allowed his love to die—and he was taking it.

As the days passed in a frenzy of movement and instruction, a slow burn of excitement grew in Kazuo's heart. Each step took him closer to his love. His lessons eventually led him into the air, where he sat in the cockpit of a Zero and soared above the base. The fires in him were searing, he almost steered the plane seaward then, but there was not enough fuel. He landed the craft and waited until at last, the morning of his sortie dawned softly around him. When the old man came to wake him, Kazuo was ready.

He knew that his plane had only enough fuel to get him to his target. He knew that he was not allowed to turn back unless, for some reason, he would not be able to strike his target. Kazuo strapped himself into the cockpit, politely declined the offer of shackles to keep him in his seat. There was no need. They saw it in his eyes as they waved him off. This one would not fail.

At first light Kazuo had written out his will. It was no more than a few lines to tell his mother and father that he was proud to die for his country and to ask them to visit him at Yasakuni Shrine. Unlike the others, he carried no keepsake, no hand-sewn doll was strapped to his vest. He did not believe that his spirit would ever reach the shrine. Kazuo was alone with his Zero and there was nothing in front of him but the wide, blue sky. He dropped no flowers as he departed; only the vision of Soryu bloomed in his mind. *I'm coming,* he shouted as his plane soared into the clouds.

When his target appeared below him, he did exactly as he had been instructed and aimed his plane at the deck of the ship. As he approached, enemy fire ripped past the Zero, shook it in the air, but Kazuo was unconcerned. He knew that his mission would be a success. This enemy was powerless to stop him. The deck swept up below him, Kazuo tensed as the Zero swayed and he was certain he heard the sound of steel being ripped from her tail. None of it mattered. The time was at hand—as the deck sped towards his falling craft, he wrenched the wheel and directed the Zero starboard. The fire from below increased, but Kazuo was a demon of the air. The enemy could only watch in horror as he came ever closer to their ship.

At the last minute, when the enemy thought all was lost, Kazuo made a sharp dive away from the ship. Men watched in shock as the Zero crashed into the waves in what appeared to be a deliberate maneuver on the part of the pilot. For Kazuo, the moment was at hand. His stunt *was* deliberate, and as the Zero dove into the sea, Kazuo was cheering.

Beneath the waves, something stirred among the coral.

The Zero, filling rapidly with water, finally lost speed below the waves and began a slow, spiraling descent towards the bottom of the sea. Inside the cockpit, Kazuo shook himself free of the straps holding him in position. Outside the windows, the sea passed by in a haze of silent shapes as fish scattered beside the sinking craft. It was a long way down, but at last Kazuo felt the Zero settle. He climbed out of the pit and saw, to his amazement, that the plane had come to rest among a bed of white coral that spread about him as far as his eyes could see. The coral gave off a soft, white light that illuminated what seemed to be a small doorway some short distance away.

Kazuo, who had never learned to swim, found movement easy in the sea. He propelled himself forward, towards the door, and slipped through it. There, laid out on a bed of moss, was the body of Soryu. Her kimono was torn and hung from her pale shoulders. He gently reached out and pulled the fabric up to cover her flesh. Her hair was disheveled, strands of it swirled around her face, obscuring her features, tracing patterns around her neck. Kazuo swept some of it away, but he could not stop the ebb of the waters and it only drifted back across her eyes when he withdrew his hand.

He reasoned that since he had found his love, the gods who had taken her must also be nearby. He left Soryu's side reluctantly and followed a passage that led away from her bed. Soon enough, a god found him.

"What are you doing here?" A voice boomed through the corridor, shook the very walls and stopped Kazuo where he stood. He looked around but could see no one.

"I said, what are you doing here?"

Kazuo trembled. "I have come for Soryu. I will fight any who would try to keep her from me!" The fires rose in him again. He would not let this voice stand in his way.

"You dare to challenge the sea?" The voice boomed even more loudly around Kazuo.

"If the sea would keep her from me, then it is the sea I challenge." Kazuo was firm. He had not come so far to turn back at the first sign of difficulty.

"Boy, who are you?"

Kazuo straightened his shoulders. "I am Kazuo, of the Special Attack Force, and I have hit my target."

Laughter sounded in Kazuo's ears, filled the corridor, caused the water to roil and push Kazuo to and fro, but he stood his ground. A great rumbling began in the depths of the coral palace and suddenly, a large dragon took shape before Kazuo's eyes.

"You have missed your target, Kazuo of the Special Attack Force. I am standing right here." Ryujin shook his head and the scales along his body rippled in the waters.

"Then let us fight. I will not leave here without Soryu." Kazuo, who had flown a plane into the sea, still did not understand what it was to be afraid.

Ryujin laughed again. "Why will you risk your spirit for her? Wouldn't you be happier at Yasakuni with the rest of your kind? You do not belong here, beneath the waves."

"I belong with Soryu. That is all I know."

"We shall see," said the dragon. "Your spirit interests me. You chose to disobey your orders for a chance to be with your love. Let us see if Soryu would do the same for you. We will let her make her choice, just as you made yours. If she chooses to be with you, I will return you both to the world above, where you may live out your lives as you see fit. If she does not, you forfeit your spirit to me." Ryujin slowly made his way past a confused Kazuo. This was not the heroic victory Kazuo had imagined, but all he could do was follow Ryujin back to Soryu's side.

He watched carefully as the dragon bent its head over the form of Soryu, still lying as though she were asleep on her bed of moss. Ryujin breathed gently on her face, Kazuo saw her stir as though she were slowly coming to consciousness, and then her eyes opened. They were the same deep green that he remembered. Kazuo was certain that she would choose to leave this place with him when asked.

"Soryu, you have a guest." The dragon backed away from the bed, where Soryu was easing herself upright.

Her gaze fell upon Kazuo's eager face. She raised a hand towards him, and then slowly pulled it back to her side. "I remember you," she said. "You are the man who loved me, and to whom I gave my love. I am sorry that I could not return to you."

Kazuo shook his head as the dragon looked on. "It doesn't matter now! I have come for you, Soryu. We can be together at last." Kazuo's eyes wandered over her face. They landed on the flower on her forehead and he recalled the golden chrysanthemum that had graced her bow.

"You said you would love me forever, but I did not expect you to find me here."

"What happened?" Kazuo asked. "They told us that you were sunk by the enemy. I could not understand why the gods would take you from me, and so I waited for the opportunity to strike at them and here I am."

The dragon noted that Kazuo looked pleased with himself. He smiled, but Kazuo did not notice. He only had eyes for Soryu.

"This young man came to fight me for you. He would challenge the very gods of the sea to be with you again. What do you think of that?"

Soryu frowned. "I have seen enough of fighting," she said.

"I thought as much." Ryujin stroked her hair gently, as though she were a child. "I offered a challenge of a different sort. The boy has done all manner of extraordinary things to be with you, Soryu, but I suggested that the choice be left to you. Would you leave this place and return with him to the world above?"

"Come on," Kazuo said. "We'll have a little house by the sea and live happily until the end of our days. I love you, Soryu."

Soryu did not immediately answer as Kazuo thought she would. Instead, she sat calmly on her bed and gazed at him as though she hardly knew his face. "Do you know why I was created?" she finally asked him.

Kazuo thought it was a curious question. "You were designed to be the best carrier we had, you were the glory of our empire, you are the Green Dragon that could outrun the waves."

Her lips curved up in a tiny smile. "You make it sound so simple, but you have not answered my question. I asked you, for what purpose was I created?" Her eyes never left his face as she spoke and inside himself, Kazuo began to feel the first stirrings of uncertainty.

"You were created to destroy the enemy." Kazuo scratched his head. He didn't understand why she was asking him these questions, but his love for her drew the answers out of his mouth.

"And did I fulfill my duty as my creators expected of me? Did I destroy the enemy?"

"You were responsible for many great victories, yes." Kazuo was growing more confused by the minute.

"And you, what became of you after I fell?"

Kazuo smiled proudly. "I volunteered for the Special Attack Force."

"Why was this force created?" Soryu's eyes burned into his.

"To destroy the enemy, of course." Kazuo felt the cold of the ocean seeping into his skin. "Have you made your decision, my love?" he asked in return.

"Yes, I think I have, but before I announce it, I would like to ask you one more thing."

"Please," said Kazuo. "Anything at all."

"Did you fulfill your duty to the men who asked this of you? Who trained you? Did you destroy the enemy?" Soryu's eyes gleamed in the soft light of the coral as strands of her hair caressed her cheek.

Kazuo felt a twist in his stomach, as though something that had lived there for many years was only now beginning to make itself known. He became angry at the woman in front of him.

"What does it matter?" he almost shouted. "All that I have done was for the love of you."

"Kazuo, dear Kazuo." Soryu smiled and again he saw a hint of sorrow in her eyes; this time he recognized it. "Love and duty are two different things. We are fortunate when they come together, but when they do not, we must sacrifice one for the other. Who would I be had I not fulfilled my obligations? I would not then be worthy of your love."

"What are you saying?" Kazuo felt the thing in his stomach rise up to overwhelm him. He was afraid for the first time in his life—not of any enemy, but of the choice Soryu was about to make.

"I will not go with you when you leave here, Kazuo. I love you, but my duty is not yet done."

"What? Your duty? You were sunk! You have no duty now." Kazuo saw the mouth of Ryujin open wide.

"Oh, but I do. I may have been sunk, but I can still serve my purpose."

"The choice has been made," Ryujin's voice again sounded in the coral palace, blotting out all thought. Soryu smiled one last time at Kazuo, and then stretched out on her bed of moss and closed her eyes. Ryujin turned towards the trembling Kazuo.

"Now, boy, you belong to me." The dragon raised its head and began to draw the water into its mouth, catching Kazuo in the current. Finally, Kazuo knew fear. It was not what he had expected. It was not the visceral fear of those confronting an enemy, it was the certain fear of those who suddenly realize that their greatest sacrifice was meaningless after all. Kazuo fell into darkness as Ryujin swallowed him whole.

A short time later, his eyes opened. He was in the Zero, arcing towards an enemy ship that drifted calmly on the sea, as though waiting for him. The bloom that was Soryu faded and fell on the floor of Kazuo's heart as another flower opened. He closed his eyes and let his Zero fall like a blossom onto the deck below, where it exploded in a profusion of petals that scattered over the waves.

Beneath the water, Soryu caught one in her hand.

THE RENTAL SISTER

ROBERT JOSEPH LEVY

I'M KIND OF KNOWN FOR telling this story, and don't worry, it's a quick one. Okay? This was the summer before I discovered acting and moved to the States, when I was still Shinju instead of Shannon. I was living in the Aoyama district, waitressing on and off and pretty much lost in life, working at an Italian restaurant at the time. There's little to no tipping in Japan—only from tourists, really—and I was complaining one day to my coworker Yoshiko about how I was having trouble paying my bills. That was the moment she suggested I make some money on the side as a rental sister.

I had to ask what this was and the answer was surprising and has to do with the hikikomori. That basically means withdrawal, and it's part of a big problem in Japan, what you would call a social epidemic. The hikikomori, almost all young men, close themselves off in their rooms for years and years, only coming out in the middle of the night to grab food before going back inside. It's like the way anorexia is here, you know, very popular? Anyway, once the family runs out of options, there are a few very expensive treatment companies that you can contract, and they send over a girl known as a rental sister, who goes to your house to try to slowly draw the boy out into the world. Yoshiko worked for Fresh Start, which was one of these companies. She said it was easy work and that she would be happy to refer me.

"Oh, and if they give you Koji Tanabashi in Meguro as your first," she said as she wrote down the address of the company, "don't tear your hair out over it." I didn't ask what she meant.

Once I applied and was accepted at Fresh Start, I immediately started my training as a rental sister. It's not like being a therapist or even an outreach worker, they told me, more like just a friend to talk to. Training was basically an afternoon of practice with my supervisor Mr. Suzuki and then a manual to read that evening. As Yoshiko predicted, my first assignment was in fact a twenty-year-old man named Koji Tanabashi, my age, who lived in the Meguro district. That's in the suburbs so I took the bus out there, reading his one-page bio along the way, and also the manual, which basically was not helpful, just things not to do like do not be too flirtatious, do not be impatient, do not be aggressive, things like that.

I went to the address and found myself at the doors of a large home, two floors and very modern, or it probably was when it was built, maybe fifty years ago? Lots of concrete and very little glass, almost like an office building or a bomb shelter but instead it was a house. I rang the doorbell and Mrs. Tanabashi, who turned out to be a very impolite woman, bowed quickly and then made her way through the expansive genkan and into the main hallway that led to the staircase. I followed after her. "You are the thirty-seventh rental girl we have hired," she said in almost a whisper as we went up the steps. "Maybe you will be the one." I decided that this was her way of telling me she had already spent a great deal of money.

We passed beneath a large skylight, and I remember looking up for a moment at the darkening sky. We went down the hall to the last door, which was on the right. I turned to Mrs. Tanabashi but she had already pulled away, heading back down the stairs. I wanted to leave as well. So, okay, I thought, you can do this, it's just like meeting a very quiet new friend, and I've had those before, so why not, you know? I kneeled down on the hard wood in front of the locked door and sat in silence for a few minutes before making sure Mrs. Tanabashi wasn't watching me; then I reached into my rucksack for the manual and read from its suggestions for introductory phrases.

"Hello, Koji!" I was trying to sound fun. "My name is Shinju, can you hear me?"

Nothing.

"I was hoping I could talk to you, and I heard you were a good listener, is that true?"

More nothing.

I began to tell him about my day, about my friends, the restaurant, how I decided to join Fresh Start, except I said I joined because I liked talking with people instead of the real reason, which was because I needed the money. I tried anything I could think of that would be helpful and not aggressive, that might appeal to a hikikomori, even slipping a friendly note under the door if he preferred to communicate that way. I told him about the movie I had seen the previous week, the one I hoped to see the next, the book I was reading and how interesting it was, even reading from it for a while. Every moment as a rental sister is a race against time, for the longer a hikikomori is shut in the less likely he is to emerge.

By my watch I could see only a half hour had passed and I was already running out of things to say. I pulled his bio out of my rucksack and looked it over again, and there was nothing so very special about him I could grab onto, really just that he liked videogames and only videogames. I hate videogames because I find them addicting, you know? I would rather use that time to read a book. Anyway, I knew I had a great deal more work to do, so I kept going. Endless time. I can still picture that hallway as if I were standing in it now: the shell-lacquered credenza, the woven screen hanging beside the traditional watercolor of fisherman returning to shore, everything in its place, just so.

Once the three hours were done and there was still no reply from the other side of the door, I said goodnight and left the house. As I started heading down the path to the main street, I turned to stare back at the house, and I happened to see the heavy curtains in the windows of one of the upper rooms move for a moment before falling still. It was Koji's room, I realized, and gave a little wave and kept walking, sure that I was being watched as I went. I would have felt like a complete failure if it wasn't for seeing those curtains move. They kept me at it.

I spent the next month making three weekly visits, and I became more prepared, more determined, so that when Mrs. Tanabashi would say "Anything?" as I left each night I might eventually have something to tell her instead of simply apologizing. I really did not like this woman. Her presence was always so heavy, being in a constant state of disapproval as she was, you know? So when I became more eager to draw Koji out I had an idea and started playing videogames at home on the computer and then I would come back to his door and talk about what happened during the game. In my mind that was already better than how I was doing before, and I talked on and on, endless one-sided discussions of what I was playing, my scores, who I encountered along the way, things like that. I thought it would be my way in, but it wasn't, and I began to worry about my paycheck.

One night, though, six weeks after I first started as Koji's rental sister, something finally happened. I'd already abandoned my videogame idea, and, having nothing left to share of myself, I started making up stories to tell. I was so bored by then, sitting alone for hours on the small tatami mat I would bring with me; I was surprised that there was nothing comfortable already in place in front of Koji's door, my being the thirty-seventh sister to put herself there for hours on end. So I began talking about how I was going to move to the United States and become a famous actress and that I would take him with me and we would live in Hollywood together, just nonsense at the time. Now that I say it, I was acting even in that moment.

So I talk on and on, and then I feel something push against my hand, which is against the bottom of the door. I look down and a Post-It note has been slipped out to me, and it says

YOU ARE PRETTY

I couldn't help it. I laughed, since I was so grateful he had written anything at all, and that it wasn't to tell me to go away. "Why, thank you, Koji," I said. "You're a very nice young man. And I bet you are a handsome one as well."

After another minute he slips a second note under the door, and it says

NOT ANYMORE

"Come now, I find that hard to believe," I went on. "You're so handsome in photographs and no one loses that much beauty just by being alone." I hadn't actually seen a picture of him. There wasn't one in his bio, or anywhere in the house that I could find. And yes, I was ignoring the advice in the manual at this time, but I got through to him my own way, didn't I? "I'll tell you what. If you open the door a crack I'll tell you if you are handsome or not, okay?"

Another minute passes, then another note, and it says

I CANNOT OPEN THE DOOR

"Koji," I said, going for playfulness. "What's wrong, don't you like me anymore?"

Then, very quickly this time, another note appears, and it says

I AM COLD HERE

"Well, okay, I'll go ask your mother for a blanket and I'll leave it outside the door for you to take after I'm gone."

I went downstairs and found Mrs. Tanabashi in the kitchen, preparing her dinner; her husband was an international businessman and he was away from home a great deal. "You won't believe it!" I said, so excited to tell her of my progress. "Koji started slipping me notes." I handed them to her and as she read them her eyes went wide with shock. Then she looked up at me, and her anger was impossible to mistake.

"Wait for me in the genkan," she said, her back to me as she left the kitchen. I went to wait for her there, and it was almost an hour later—I had nothing to do but stare at the row of shoes beside the entrance—that the doorbell rang. Mrs. Tanabashi came to answer it, and it was Mr. Suzuki, my Fresh Start supervisor. He looked furious.

"Shinju," he said, "you are a very irresponsible girl and I want you to apologize to Mrs. Tanabashi."

"What have I done wrong?" I asked him, and he turned to Mrs. Tanabashi, who handed him the notes.

"What are these?" he said, holding them out to me.

"They're notes from Koji," I replied, taking them. "He slipped them under the door when we were talking."

Mr. Suzuki turned back to Mrs. Tanabashi. "I'm so sorry," he said to her. "She won't be coming back here."

"What's going on?" I said, losing my patience. "Tell me what I did."

"Enough of your lies, Shinju. I know you wrote these notes yourself."

"I would never do that!" I said. "Why would I ever do such a thing?"

"Because someone must have told you there's no one in that room." He looked down at the floor, then back at Mrs. Tanabashi, then back at me. "I'm going to have to terminate your employment, you realize."

"These notes were slipped under the door!" I said, shouting now. "There's someone on the other side!"

"There's no one in there and you know it. We use this as a facility that Mrs. Tanabashi kindly offered to Fresh Start so that new rental sisters can get practice before their real work with the hikikomori. *This* is your training, Shinju."

"But there's someone in there!" I insisted, louder this time, and then Mrs. Tanabashi let out a kind of scream of frustration that silenced me.

"Follow me, then, 'pretty' girl," she said, and Mr. Suzuki and I went after her up the stairs. When we got to the door she rudely stepped on my tatami, reaching into her pocket for a ring of keys. She struggled with the lock for a moment before the knob turned, and when she swung open the door a stack of papers on the other side spread across the floor like the opening of a fan.

The room was empty. There was no furniture, no closet, nothing but the heavy curtains rawn across the far wall. It was much smaller than I had pictured it but still I stepped inside, just to make sure, Mr. Suzuki entering after me. Nothing.

Mrs. Tanabashi left the keys in the lock and headed down the hall, slamming her bedroom door behind her.

"I don't understand," I said, staring down at the papers on the floor, the writings of thirty-seven rental sisters in training, all unread, a rainbow of different colored and sized stationeries glowing in the light from the open door. "I was so sure. Maybe if she would just look at the handwriting again—"

But Mr. Suzuki interrupted me. "Listen, Shinju, I understand that this was something you wanted to happen so badly that you created your own fantasy. But you've managed to deeply offend Mrs. Tanabashi, and that is not excusable."

"What have I done that was so wrong?" I asked him.

"The reason she offers our company this space is because her own son was a hikikomori. He landed up hanging himself. This used to be his room." I understood her in that moment, the weight of her soul, and longed to console her; I never saw her again.

And then, and this is exactly how it happened, I felt this strange coldness pass over me, almost like static electricity, you know? It felt like something was brushing against my hair, back and forth and back again, as if from above. I looked up at the ceiling.

"Time to go," Mr. Suzuki said.

I left alone, heading down the stairs and into the genkan, where I put on my shoes and went out into the cold evening air; autumn had arrived without my noticing. I stopped to stare up at Koji's windows, the heavy curtains black and unmoving, before I made my way home.

I try not to think about that stage in my life very often, days of vast emptiness waiting to be filled by something, anything that might show me my way, my purpose in being. But I think about that night all the time. In fact, I still have those notes he slipped under the door. I carry them with me in my wallet wherever I go.

Would you like to see them?

君はきれい

もうハンサムじゃない

ドアガ開けられない

僕は寒い

THE WHITE BONE FAN

RICHARD PARKS

JIN LEE HANNIGAN HAD ONLY been a goddess for a few days. It was hard enough just being herself, what with her sorry excuse for a love life and her mother bringing up the subject of grandchildren every other breath. Being a goddess just added another degree of difficulty.

Ok, Jin knew that—technically—she wasn't a goddess at all. She was a *bodhisattva*, a transcendent being known as Kuan Yin who had refused to transcend, now reborn in the all too mortal form of Jin Lee Hannigan, aged twenty-one, of Medias, Mississippi. Now the acting Buddhist Goddess of Mercy, the first two things Jin learned after her apotheosis were 1) that mercy wasn't about kindness and 2) that being a goddess was hard work. It was Kuan Yin's special charge to free souls trapped in the various hells. There were an awful lot of hells.

Now Jin was summoned. She knew she'd been summoned, because she found herself in a corridor very much like the one that had led her from Medias to the Gateway to All Hells when she first found out that little matter of her apotheosis. The same flaring torches, the same carved monsters in the stone. The same dust and debris of ages settling on the stone floor.

I don't suppose anyone ever sweeps up.

It was a silly thought, but no more silly than a corridor with torches that apparently never burned out and never needed to be replaced. Jin knew that she wasn't really in a corridor. There was nothing solid beneath her. It was an illusion. It occurred to Jin that, perhaps, illusions were not always bad things. She'd suddenly become very fond of the one that made the passageways to Hell seem like simple stone corridors that allowed her to travel infinite space in the time it took to cross Pepper Street. Jin hurried down the corridor toward the far door.

Which wasn't there. Jin simply stepped through an open arch and into a cavern not unlike that containing the Doorway to All the Hells. The main differences that Jin could see at first glance was that this one seemed more elongated than round; she couldn't even see where it ended and she was fairly certain this wasn't simply because of the dim light. The other thing she noticed was that the floor of the cavern was strewn with small rocks and looked like the bed of a dried-out river.

She frowned. "This is a hell, too?"

"I suppose. It depends on your definition."

Later Jin would think that, perhaps, she should be used to people just appearing and disappearing. As it was, she jumped back two feet and landed in a fighter's crouch in full demon form. A few feet away from her there stood a strange-looking little man. He carried a staff with several rings set into the top of it. He was bald, and his earlobes were elongated exactly as those on many of the Buddhist images Jin had seen in her studies. He was maybe five feet tall in his sandals, and wore the robes of a monk. He looked about as dangerous as a fireplug.

"Damn it all, don't *do* that!"

The little man raised his eyebrows. "Immanence, your language has certainly gotten more... colorful, since our last meeting."

Jin stood up straight and abandoned her Pulan Gong form, feeling a little foolish. She racked her brains while she waited for her heart to stop pounding. "You're... O-Jizou, yes?"

He nodded. "You remember me, after all this time. I am honored, Kannon-sama."

She was in the presence of the *bodhisattva* Jizou, known in Japan as the God of Children. Which made sense, since "Kannon" was the Japanese form of Kuan Yin. It was a good thing that some deep down part of her knew what she was supposed to be, because Jin as Jin Lee Hannigan didn't claim to be an expert on Japanese cosmology or, indeed, any other. Still, something in the way he said "honored" led Jin to think that he wasn't honored at all. In fact, if it had been anyone other than the Enlightened Being O-Jizou was supposed to be, she'd have thought he sounded downright annoyed.

"I'm in a mortal incarnation and my memory is faulty. Have I done something to offend you?"

"Lord Yama, King of the First Hell, informed me of your condition. As for offense... those in my care have suffered because of you. Suffering may be the lot of all creatures, but usually it serves a purpose, however obscure. Does what you have done serve a purpose? Yama believes so, but I don't know for certain and neither, apparently, do you."

Jin said nothing. There didn't seem to be anything *to* say. Then the moment passed and the little monk turned on his heel and set out at a walk so brisk that Jin had to run to catch up. "Follow me, please," he said over his shoulder.

"I'm *trying*," Jin said, amazed that the man's short legs could move so quickly.

They hadn't quite reached the riverbed when a fierce-looking old woman appeared out of nowhere, blocking their path. Her hair was white and her eyes jet black, and those eyes glittered like cold wet stones. "Give me your clothes," she said to Jin.

Jin put her hands on her hips. "Excuse me?"

"Begone, Datsueba," O-Jizou said. "Do you not recognize Kannon the Merciful?"

The hag looked at her even closer. "I know guilt when I see it. Her clothes belong to me. That is the Law."

"I don't think so," said Jin. In another moment she was in full demon form again. The hag didn't appear worried at all, or even surprised. She did look a little puzzled.

O-Jizou sighed. "Stop that," he said to Jin, as if she were a misbehaving child, then he turned back to the hag. "Whatever else this woman may be, she is mortal and alive. You're wasting our time, Datsueba."

"Mortal stink," said the hag finally, and made a sniffing noise. "I should have noticed. Didn't want to touch her anyway."

In another instant the hag was gone and Jin had returned to her normal appearance. O-Jizou started walking again and Jin hurried to catch up. "What was *that* all about?"

The little monk shrugged. "After their initial judgment, the dead, guilty and guiltless alike, come to this place to cross the river to the next realm. Those judged guiltless cross on a bridge. Those who are guilty must either wade or swim the river. It is the Datsueba's task to strip the clothing from the guilty."

"Just what am I supposed to be guilty of? Are all the guilty here supposed to stay naked?!"

"As to the first, I cannot say. For the second, no, they clothe themselves again in time," he said, as if the matter was of no importance.

Jin just hurried along for a little while, so intent on keeping pace with O-Jizou that the inherent absurdity of what he had said took a little while to catch up to her. When it did, she almost stopped.

"Ummm, O-Jizou, correct me if I'm wrong, but where we're walking is dry. There's no water here."

"Not a drop," O-Jizou agreed.

"So why does anyone need to wade?"

"Because they don't understand that the water is an illusion. If they did, they wouldn't belong here." Apparently seeing that Jin was about to ask something else he went on, "Even in your mortal form you should know this. Or has your Third Eye never opened?"

"Oh, right." Jin said. She did not, however, feel an overwhelming urge to open that eye just then and verify absolute reality.

As they walked along the riverbed Jin saw something very strange. All along the bank on one side were children, piling heavy stones one on top of the other. Some of them were in fact naked. Others wore tattered clothes of an overwhelming variety: kimonos, robes, jeans, dresses, jumpers. Their ages seemed to vary from those barely able to walk to pre-adolescents. All seemed to be working at the stones. Some were piling in groups, others worked alone.

"What are they doing?"

"They're too small to wade the river, or the older ones can't swim. They're piling up the stones to try and make a footpath to the other side."

"I don't understand. What can children so young be guilty of?"

O-Jizou just shrugged again. "Ask the one who judges them."

Even as they spoke Jin saw a ragged boy turn away to pick up another heavy stone and in that moment a small demon almost identical to the one on Joyce's shoulder dashed out of nowhere and shoved the pile of stones, scattering them and reducing the pile to nothing. The demon vanished before the child could return with the stone to find all his work gone to nothing.

"The poor thing—"

Jin had started to turn back but without even looking at her O-Jizou had reached back and taken hold of her wrist. "Neither you nor your pity can help him, Kannon. Please concentrate on those who need you."

As scoldings went this one was very gentle, but it was a scolding none the less. Jin wanted to be angry, but couldn't. "This is what you deal with all the time, isn't it?" she asked.

"Yes."

"Can… can you do anything for them?"

"When the time comes—and not before—I help them cross the river."

"How do you know when the time comes?"

"How do you free someone from hell?" he returned, mildly. "It is, as the King of the First Hell has taken to saying lately, 'my job,' just as freeing the punished is yours."

"So I've been reminded. A lot," Jin said dryly.

"If it were not so, then His Majesty would not be doing *his* job."

That sounded like a scolding too. Jin sighed. "If it turns out that this incarnation is a mere whim of mine—and your guess on this is as good as my own—I'll be sure to apologize for wasting everyone's time. In the meantime can we just drop the subject of my incarnation?"

He just shrugged. "Your incarnation does not matter."

"Then why do you keep bringing it up?"

Somewhat to Jin's surprise, O-Jizou actually seemed to be thinking about her question as they walked. "I don't know," he said finally. "Maybe I'm just angry."

"Human emotion is an illusion," Jin said, even though she wasn't really convinced of that herself.

"'Show me someone who's never been bewitched by a pair of beautiful eyes and I'll show you a stone buddha,'" replied O-Jizou, smiling.

"Is that a real saying, or did you just make it up?"

"Yes," he said.

O-Jizou smiled again and Jin started to wonder if she was beginning to like the guy. She really could do without the scolding, though. Neither said anything for a time. Jin followed the little monk up a narrow path on the opposite side of the dry river bed from the children. The land on the other side of the river didn't look very different from the river bed itself: it was flat, stony, and dry.

"What happens when a child finally crosses the river? Or is that something I should already know?"

"Of course it is but, since you don't, I'll tell you—then the child goes where it's supposed to go, just like anyone else who crossed over. Or rather, the child goes where it needs to go. I can't explain it any better than that. I can, however, show you. We're approaching Mariko's—"

He didn't even get to finish. The air in front of them shimmered like one of the doors to the hell corridors and everything changed from one step to the next. One moment they walked in a dry, desolate place and in the next they were strolling down a narrow forest path in autumn. To either side of the path were maples in the full russet display marking the end of summer. There was a cool but not unpleasant edge to the breeze that made the pines whisper and the maple leaves rustle. They came to a place where a mossy stone bridge crossed a quiet dark stream, and there they stopped.

Jin knew that the way the place looked was not real, any more than the river keeping the children from crossing into their next destination was real. And yet, like that river, the appearance of the path was important. This seemingly tranquil place looked the way it looked for a reason, and that reason belonged to neither herself nor O-Jizou who, without preamble, had just sat down cross-legged under the larger of the two maples flanking the path about fifty feet from the bridge. He placed his staff across his knees and just sat there, not looking at her. He was looking over the bridge. After a moment Jin did the same and saw the figure approaching from the opposite side.

"Mariko?" Jin asked, and he grunted assent.

She wore a kimono of pure white, and it contrasted with hair blacker even than Jin's, and far longer. It trailed in two long braids down the front of her kimono almost to her waist; the rest spread from her head to fall down around her shoulders and black almost like a cape. Her face was in shadow but, by what Jin could see, it was almost as white as the kimono. She knew that Japanese women at certain times in history had painted their faces white, so thought little of it at first.

If Mariko noticed either of them she didn't show it. She started across the bridge with the tiny, shuffling steps that a formal kimono demanded. Jin had worn one once in a school play and couldn't understand how anybody could walk more than a few steps in the silly things, but Mariko managed just fine. She stopped at the highest point of the wooden bridge and looked down, gazing at the dark water, her long, graceful fingers resting on top of the railing.

Jin had been waiting, in a sense, for the other shoe to drop, but when it did she still felt a little sick. Mariko's fingers on the railing. Fingers too long, too thin. Jin remembered what little she had seen of Mariko's face and finally put it all together.

The skeleton is wearing a kimono. Jin almost giggled, though she didn't really think it was funny. She wasn't frightened—she had seen far worse in her crash course in being Kuan

Yin—but the sight was at once shocking and pitiful and for several long moments Jin could do nothing at all put stare at the poor girl, who still seemed oblivious to all except the water. When she finally did look up from the stream Jin thought for a moment that she'd finally noticed them, but soon realized that Mariko was looking down the path the way they had come. Jin glanced back that way but she saw nothing and it was clear that Mariko saw the same. The poor creature's shoulders raised briefly and lowered; Jin would have sworn the girl had sighed, even though she had neither lungs nor breath to do so.

O-Jizou made a slight noise, little more than a clearing of his throat, but Jin knew what it really meant—her cue. Jin headed for the bridge, even though as yet she didn't have the slightest idea what she was going to do, and understanding that it was her nature to sort just such things out didn't make her feel the least bit more confident.

The understanding that Mariko was little more than a skeleton in a white kimono bothered Jin just a little, and not for the obvious reason. If all hells were personal—and Jin knew that to be true—then the particular torment, experience, and appearance of the punished one were all personal as well. Yet here was little more than an assemblage of bones and scraps of cloth pretending to be, as Jin perceived her, a young girl of about seventeen. Why? Jin could understand if Mariko was at a place where she would be subjected to horror and revulsion at her appearance; that was a torment that made sense, and Jin could look for understanding there. Yet Mariko was alone. Here there was no one to see her bones, her sorry pretense at being a living girl, so what was the point of it? It's not as if the girl carried a mirror to look at herself; so far as Jin could see she only carried a delicate fan tucked into her sash, and considering the height of the bridge it was unlikely the water below could cast a reflection plain enough for Mariko to see.

Perhaps she merely wants it to be clear that she has died...but clear to whom?

Jin approached the bridge and Mariko didn't react. It was only when she stepped onto the wooden walkway that Mariko turned to look at her.

"Saburo—" Mariko stopped. She sounded confused. "You're not Saburo-sama," she said, staring at her with the black holes where her eyes should be.

Jin took another step. "No. My name is Jin."

Mariko took a step back. "What are you doing here? Did Saburo-sama send you?"

"You're waiting on Saburo, aren't you?" Jin asked, dodging the question like a hurled stone. She took another step. So did Mariko, in the opposite direction.

"Stay back!"

Jin paused, her hand still on the railing. "I'm not going to hurt you."

Mariko shook her head slowly. "I know who you are. I won't go."

"Go where?"

The question seemed to confuse Mariko. "Where Saburo-sama isn't," she said finally.

"It would seem to me," Jin said dryly, "that *this* is a place where Saburo-sama isn't. How long have you been waiting?"

Silence, then Jin saw tears forming at the corners of Mariko's fleshless eyes. The idea that this was an impossible thing to happen came and was dismissed in a moment; it happened, so obviously it was not impossible. Not at that place, at least.

For a moment Mariko's fear and suspicion deserted her. "I'm so tired," she said. Tears glistened on the bones of her face. "Please go away."

"Who do you think I am, Mariko san?"

"You are Blessed Kannon. You do not look as I expected, but it is you, I am certain."

Jin nodded. "You're an interesting girl, Mariko-san. I don't think you're confused at all about where you are and who you are. Yet you tarry here wearing a face like death itself waiting for someone who is never going to come. What was this 'Saburo-sama' to you?"

"Everything," Mariko said. "And he *will* come. We could not marry, but he said we would be re-united and we will. When that happens, he will see that I kept faith with him!"

Jin had a pretty good idea of what Mariko meant by that, but this was not the time for guesswork. She had to be sure. "Mariko, take my hand."

The ghost-girl took another step back. "I won't!"

"I'm trying to help you, Mariko, but I can't unless you help me, too. I promise I will not drag you away from here if you really don't want to go."

Expression was hard to read on the face of a skull, but Jin was sure Mariko was doubtful. "Well..."

"Kannon does not lie," Jin said.

Reluctantly, Mariko extended her bony hand and Jin grasped it gently. She felt none of the revulsion she had half-way expected to feel.

She saw what Mariko saw, felt what Mariko felt. In that instant she *was* Mariko as she had been a thousand years before. She stood on a small bridge in the garden of her father's house. Her father emerged from a small tea hut father down the path, and he had a guest. Jin felt her heart beating faster at the sight of the handsome young man accompanying him. Her normally gruff father was in a surprisingly good mood and he smiled at her.

"Daughter, come greet our guest."

As Mariko/Jin and Saburo bowed to each other, for a moment their eyes met. In that moment Jin finally knew what it was like to fall in love because, in the mind and spirit of a girl dead for a thousand years, for the first time and yet again she did fall in love. The sadness was almost more than she could bear. The details came flooding into her, filling in the small gaps that, to Jin, already seemed like a completed picture: Mariko was a girl of good family who fell in love with a scholar visiting her father's house. They spent one blissful night together but he was promised to another and told her so. In a moment Jin knew all this and more beside, no more or less than what she needed to know. When the vision ended Jin knew it was still up to her to put the pieces into place because her previous view of the matter was askew in one very crucial area.

Jin glanced at the ornate paper fan in her sash, its outer spokes of white bone. "That was Saburo-sama's token to you, wasn't it?"

Mariko tugged her hand free and placed it protectively over the fan. "He will see that I have kept faith. I've waited for him here, he will see—"

"The face you have chosen to show him. He will see your death. You didn't always wear this face, even after you came here, did you?"

"I-I don't remember."

"Oh, yes you do. Death doesn't come again to one already dead, but time still exists for all who cannot remove themselves from it, and you've waited a long time indeed. You became very angry with Saburo-sama over the years, didn't you? It was then that you started to let the memory of flesh fall away and now you're not waiting for him at all. You're waiting to show Saburo-sama what he did to you!"

Mariko didn't say anything, but she didn't have to. Jin smiled at her. "Break the fan, Mariko-chan. Let it go."

Mariko closed both skeletal hands around the precious fan and hugged it to her chest as if to protect it from Jin. "I won't! I will wait..."

Jin shook her head, slowly. "Did it never occur to you that maybe you misunderstood? You're not waiting on Saburo—he's waiting on you."

Mariko just stared at her for a moment. "What are you talking about?"

"Saburo never understood what he meant to you. He didn't get word of your suicide until he returned to his father's house where his new bride was waiting for him. Because of his obedience to his father he tried to forget you but never managed, and that regret has followed him across the River of Souls numerous times since then."

"So why has he not come to me here?"

"Because he *can't*! This is not a meeting place. It is only where you wait for what will never happen while Saburo lives out his lives without the potential of settling matters between you, because you hide in this place."

"That's not true..." Mariko began, but Jin didn't let her finish.

"Kannon does not lie," Jin repeated. "Either break the fan or I will. Your choice."

"No you won't," Mariko said in triumph. "You promised!"

"I promised not to drag you from this place if you didn't really want to go. You do want to go, Mariko."

"No I don't! I will wait forever!"

"You don't have forever, Mariko. Sooner or later you will settle matters with Saburo, because you must. You've delayed that long enough. You've punished Saburo enough."

"No," she said, and that was all.

"You've got every right to be angry," Jin said gently, "But do you really never want to see Saburo again? If you can honestly say so, Mariko, I will leave you here. Only, for your own sake, tell the truth."

"I..." Mariko's voice trailed off. She seemed puzzled again, and in that moment Mariko's manner changed, and for a moment, Jin saw the face in Mariko's memory, her true face, and then it was gone again, replaced with something much colder and harder than bone

"He can rot in whatever Hell comes to him," Mariko said then. "I will not go — "

Jin took the fan. She never took her gaze from the ruined face, but Jin's right hand snaked out and snatched the fan from between Mariko's bony fingers. Before Mariko could even react, Jin snapped the fan in half.

"You *will* go, Mariko," Jin said. "It's time."

Mariko howled like an enraged animal and lunged. Jin grabbed Mariko's wrists and held on as the girl snarled and tried to bite Jin with her skull full of teeth. Jin held her there with more calm than she felt. In a moment Mariko's bones clothed themselves with the memory of flesh just long enough to smile a little wistfully at Jin.

"I know," she said. In a few more moments she was gone, along with the bridge and the river and everything that had to do with Mariko's time and place.

She was hunkered down on the bank of the river of souls, her head resting on her knees, glaring at nothing, when O-Jizou found her again.

"Why is the Goddess of Mercy so angry?" he asked.

"I don't know. Maybe I'm getting tired of destroying people's dreams. Even if they are nightmares most of the time."

O-Jizou nodded slightly. "You'll get used to it."

"How do you know that?"

"Because you always do. For now and on Mariko's behalf, I thank you."

"For doing my job?" Jin asked, a little shortly.

"For helping her," he said.

Jin just sighed, and then she nodded. "I'll try to remember that."

On her way back to Medias Jin passed through the central cavern know as "The Gateway to All the Hells." On a central dais stood a gigantic golden statue of Kannon the Merciful, smiling faintly at her.

"Your job sucks, you know," Jin said.

Across time from the Kannon that Was and the Kuan Yin that Is, Jin heard her own answer come back to her.

I KNOW.

THE TEARS OF MY MOTHER, THE SHELL OF MY FATHER

EUGIE FOSTER

I DID NOT DWELL OVERMUCH UPON destiny, living among the priests in Oda, sweeping the steps of the *jinja* shrine, and meditating at the seashore. Until the morning the Heikegani crab with the face of a samurai etched in its sepia armor came ashore and spoke to me.

As was my habit in those summer days, I had risen to greet the dawn. Hime, my white, four-legged shadow, tagged at my heels, more fascinated by the lapping waves than she ever was by a scampering mouse or the wings of a bird—a proclivity which ensured her welcome among the life- and peace-loving priests: a death-colored cat that never killed. Kneeling on the rocky beach that bordered the shrine, I faced the northeast expanse of endless waves. The first threads of silver brushed the horizon as fingers of water swept the shore. They curled into soft fists and retreated, leaving behind the crab.

It was large for its kind, its carapace as wide as my outstretched palm. Hime curled her tail around her paws as it scuttled from the water, her golden eyes impassive. I envied her composure. The crab approached with far greater alacrity than the dawn's warmth, and I scrambled from my posture of meditation.

It did not menace me, but rather tilted its shell so I was treated to the visage of the scowling samurai on its back. I had never credited the stories that linked these creatures to the ghosts of the Taira who died in the Battle of Dan-no-ura—although I was scrupulous never to eat their meat—but never before had the shell formations seemed so lifelike.

The flat eyes blinked open, transforming from the hard curve of burnished almond to the liquid and living orbs of a man. They fixed upon me, and the shell-sculpted lips rippled apart.

"Boy, I did not die so you could languish among the priests, contemplating rocks and trees."

The crab used the high speech of the courts in the manner of a lord to an inferior. I was so astonished that I did not think to be offended.

"Honorable, er, crab, I apologize if I have somehow wronged you—" I began.

The carapace-face scowled. "To think my son would grow to be such a simpering weakling. It took a fearsome oni demon to finish me, and your mother fought like a tigress that you might live."

I gaped at the crab. "Son?"

The face's expression softened. "Perhaps it is the priests I should blame. Nevertheless, the time for indolence is over. In three days it will be the anniversary of our murders. If you would honor we who bore you, go to your mother and staunch her tears."

"M-my mother?" I had never known the comfort of a mother. I had been surrendered as a squalling infant to the kindly, albeit reserved, care of the priests.

"They hewed off her feet so she could not run. Now she stands on Mount Mori, telling her tale to all. Free her and avenge me before the sun dawns on the fourth day, or I will curse you as a faithless son."

The crab swiveled and marched back into the dappled waters. As we conversed, the dawn had transformed into morning. Adorned with glittering jewels of sunlight, the sea crested over the samurai's helm, erasing dimension, color, and expression from the drab shell. In a spray of brine, the crab sank into the depths and was gone.

I stared for long moments where I had last seen the animated visage of a father I had never known. Hime groomed a creamy paw as though nothing had transpired more momentous than sunrise. She miaoed, and it shook me from my stupor.

I pelted back to the shrine, leaving Hime to complete her feline ablutions.

Kannushi Akio was making offerings to the *kami* as I burst into the *jinja's* heart. Although I all but danced with impatience, he continued pouring a trickle of *omiki*, ritually purified *sake*, into a pottery dish, before turning to acknowledge me.

He bowed, and with belated decorum, I returned the courtesy.

"Hiroki-kun," he said, "I see from your sandals that you did not choose to wade in the tide pools this morning. Were they not as enticing as yesterday's?"

Remorse suffused my face. In my agitation, I had blundered into this sacred space without removing my footwear.

"Sensei, forgive me." I wobbled, balancing on one leg as I struggled to undo the laces of my *waraji*.

He padded past me in immaculate socks, his feet silent over the shrine's floor. I hopped after him, one sandal dangling from my hand and the other still affixed to my foot.

"A crab spoke to me," I blurted as he paused at the shoe cupboard to retrieve his own *waraji*.

He seated himself on the entranceway's raised ledge to better don his sandals. "What did it say?"

Akio was my favorite priest. Although the eldest of the brotherhood—his face creased and seamed as ancient parchment—he was the only one who would tie up the hem of his robes to splash in the sea with a young boy and who always had time to hear me with a solemn face and boundless patience, whether I was complaining about the prevalence of pickled eel at dinnertime or musing about the nature of the infinite. But now I wished he would register disbelief to better match my turmoil.

"It said it was my father's spirit. It told me it would curse me if I did not comfort my mother who cries without feet on the mountain. But that's ridiculous, isn't it? It was a Heikegani crab, and surely I'm not descended from the Taira clan."

Waraji neatly affixed, Akio rose and strolled outside. I hobbled after him, admonishing myself for my single-shoed predicament—both for taking off the one and forgetting to replace it when I had the opportunity.

In the shadowed canopy of a copse of elm trees, Akio settled into an attitude of serenity. I plunked myself beside him and hurriedly laced on my detached *waraji*.

"Why are you so certain that you cannot be Taira?" he asked. "Have you had so many encounters with talking crabs that you have determined they are prone to uttering falsehoods?"

"B-but, I can't be nobly born. I'm nobody of consequence."

"You are as you have always been. The circumstances of your birth cannot grant or detract consequence."

"But—"

"Your given name is Taira no Chikazane. Your father was Taira no Sukemori, the second son of Taira no Shigemori, who was the first son and heir of Taira no Kiyomori, directly descended from Emperor Kuammu himself."

Each of his words penetrated like icy raindrops. "Why have you never told me of my heritage?"

"Would you have me send you into the world with only a single sandal?" Akio tapped my newly-donned *waraji*. "As you have demonstrated, all actions must occur in their proper sequence. Omitting or neglecting any of the prescribed elements results in shame, imbalance, and disharmony." My sock, visible as it protruded over the straw toe, was begrimed from my clumsy pursuit from shrine to copse.

"My family's honor is more than a mishap of footwear!"

"Exactly."

I waved my hand, seeking to dispel the cloud of confusion Akio's words had created. "The crab said my mother wept on the mountainside. But it also said they were both murdered."

"A perplexing riddle. I have found that the best means of unraveling an enigma is by meditation. Truth typically reveals itself once one has achieved enough clarity to perceive it."

He closed his eyes.

"Sensei, I can't just sit here and meditate. I must go to Mount Mori."

"As you will, Hiroki-kun. But do bring along your book of sutras and a calligraphy brush so you may continue your studies. I also recommend you take a jar of *omiki*. *Sake* is so refreshing after a long trek." His hand dipped into his sleeve and pulled out a slender, porcelain container. "How convenient that I poured an extra jar this morning."

I accepted the rice wine, bemused and exasperated. "Thank you, Sensei."

He cracked an eye open. "And put on clean socks before you go."

It seemed foolish to collect those things Akio had suggested, pointless delay. If I had not been in the habit of obeying him, I would have marched myself off without hesitation. In frenzied haste I retrieved brush and book and donned a clean pair of socks. As I pulled them on, Hime appeared.

"I must go off to perform the duty my father commanded," I told her. "But don't worry. I'm sure the priests will fill your bowl with fish and rice every day."

Duly outfitted, I set off for the *torii*, the shrine's physical and metaphysical gate. However, I discovered that Hime had no intention of letting me embark alone upon my mission. She sidled at my legs, ignoring my efforts to shoo her—both cajoling and scolding alike. Reasoning with a cat is as futile as arguing with the waves, and rather than waste more time, I gave up. Thus, Hime padded beside me as I ascended that grandfather spirit steeped in age and grandeur, Mount Mori.

We trekked the slender trail while the sun slipped from the eastern gates and wheeled across the palace of sky. As the sun retreated into her western pavilion, I cleared the debris from a ditch, our shelter for the night. It occurred to me—belly rumbling and teeth chattering—that in my hurry, I had neglected to provision myself with so much as a rice ball or tinder box.

Hime did not immediately chastise me for my blunder. First she miaoed politely, inquiring after supper. But when I showed her the emptiness of my sleeves, her cries turned plaintive.

"Forgive me, gentle one. Tonight, you and I must go hungry. But as soon as it's dawn, I will look for a stream to fish. Come, curl up in my arms; at least I can endeavor to warm you."

Hime fixed me with her golden eyes and, quick as only a cat can, bounded away. I debated for a heartbeat whether I should let her go and trust her to return. But Hime was a pampered creature, unfamiliar with wilderness dangers. I would never forgive myself if she came to harm.

I chased after. Fortunately, a white cat's coat is well suited to catching stray beams of moonlight, and I glimpsed her stalking through the underbrush.

"Hime-chan, come here," I called. But, in the infuriating manner of catkind, she allowed me to approach only close enough to tantalize before leaping away. She led me a merry chase, crashing through prickly scrub and wending through dense foliage. At last, I saw her crouched atop a boulder. Around her perch, a stream rippled, mirror-bright.

With detached amusement, Hime let me pluck her from her roost. I had every intention of scolding her, but the notion fled when I saw the woman standing in the stream.

She was beautiful, her inky hair flowing in a mantle down her back. Her kimono was embroidered brocade patterned with elegant butterflies. But where her legs should be were trailing wisps of nothing. Tears coursed from her empty eyes, mingling with the smoke and mist of her absent legs, to join with the scrolling stream.

"Come closer," she whispered, "so you may hear my tale."

I did not move, only clutched Hime tighter. "Noble lady, I can hear you well enough from here."

"Then listen. When the oni came, my husband bade me run so that I and our son might live. But it was to death I fled. Treachery and assassins, they spilled my life on this stone. My last sight was of a black-garbed killer turning to slay my baby. Husband and child murdered. I am doomed to an eternity of sorrow."

I swallowed. "Who was your husband?"

"The noble samurai, Taira no Sukemori."

"Then you need no longer mourn for your son. He was given to priests to be raised and is in good health, notwithstanding an empty belly."

"Liar! For shame, to taunt a grieving mother. Your disrespect has earned you a yurei's curse!"

"Would you damn the son you gave your life to save?"

The yurei of my mother studied me, still weeping black tears. "Prove you are he, and I will depart for the Pure Land and give you my blessing instead."

"Very well. What proof would you credit?"

"Only the reverence a son owes the memory of his mother." She clasped her hands in the sleeves of her kimono and waited.

The reverence a son owes the memory of his mother? Unnerved by the yurei's wet, unblinking stare, I contemplated the boulder. Such an ominous rock, not like the sacred stones that adorned the shrine's provinces. The thought of my mother's spirit anchored here, chained by violence and tragedy, weighted my heart. Maybe I could not free her, and perhaps she would curse me for my presumption, but I would be comforted, knowing that the boulder, at least, had been honorably consecrated.

I had not taken priestly vows yet, but I had attended many purification ceremonies, and thanks to Akio, I had a jar of *omiki*. And did not the priests say that a single, sincere prayer could move heaven?

I tore several empty pages from my sutra book, ripped and folded them into lightning-shaped *shide* streamers, and bound them with grass to the handle of my calligraphy brush to craft a makeshift *shide* wand. Bowing to the world's corners, I strove for tranquility.

"Heavenly *kami* and earthly *kami*," I intoned, "hear me." My hands trembled as I flicked the *shide* wand over the boulder. "Purity of Heaven, purity of Earth, sweep impurities from within and without." The *shide* rustled and shushed, a familiar sound, holy and restful. "I beseech the *kami* to cleanse and bless this place so my mother may know peace." I bowed and unstoppered the jar of *omiki*. My hands no longer shook as I poured the *sake* onto the boulder. "Reverently, I speak this prayer. *Kashikomi kashikomi mo maosu*."

When I was done, my mother's yurei raised her head to the starry sky. Her eyes were bright as hope, and she no longer wept.

"Surely, only a dutiful son would forgo food and drink to bring *omiki* to honor the place of his mother's death," she murmured. "I am content. What will you do now, Chikazane-kun?"

"My father's spirit called upon me to avenge him. I must kill the oni that murdered him."

A tiny crease appeared on my mother's brow. "It is the hasty hunter who lunges for the rustling bush before he knows what it conceals." She bowed. "Or the hungry one. At least I can keep your clamoring belly from clouding your caution. But beware that your true quarry does not elude you as you chase after a paper tiger."

I opened my mouth, abuzz with questions, but a bubble of light whirled from the heavens, stealing away breath, words, and opportunity. It whispered around my mother, playing with the hem of her kimono as it bore her aloft. She glanced back, and the expression on her face was both tender and pensive.

"Chikazane-kun, follow the stream up the mountain," she called, "and you will find the oni's cave and perhaps the steel beneath the paper."

Then she was gone.

Where she had been, a ball of flame danced on the water. It glided across the surface and settled atop the newly-sanctified boulder. While I gaped, it flared bright as fifty lanterns, and before I could raise a hand to shield my dazzled eyes, it shrank to a comforting blaze. At the base of the boulder, a sumptuous banquet had materialized: roasted fish, steamed rice, and plum wine.

Enticed by the aroma, Hime bounded to the feast. A well-mannered cat, she awaited my attendance before commencing her meal, but she made her impatience clear by the anxious lash of her tail.

I was not so amazed as to require Hime to wait longer; I hurried to join her.

The fish was delicious, each mouthful a harmony of subtle flavors and delicate textures. The rice was perfectly cooked, neither too sticky nor too dry, and the plum wine was refinement itself. As we ate, the flame imparted an atmosphere of cheery hospitality and restful warmth. Despite having no fuel but the stone at its base, it seemed capable of burning indefinitely. At the completion of our meal, lulled by a sated belly, the cozy fire, and Hime purring at my side, I slept.

My dreams were filled with terrifying images of blue-skinned demons, barbed fangs glittering as they lunged at me. The murky gauze of dawn brushing my eyelids was a welcome reprieve.

Although the fire still burned, merry and warm, I shivered, chilled by my nightmares. Roused by my agitation, Hime opened her eyes and yawned.

"Ah, Hime, it is all good and well for my father's spirit to exhort me to confront an oni, but I do not even possess a *katana*." I stood, and Hime grudgingly rose to her paws. "Not that I could wield one. And this oni defeated my father, a mighty samurai. How am I to keep from being devoured, much less avenge him?"

"Master, please forgive this one's presumption, but neither *Kannushi* Akio nor your mother's spirit held any delusions as to your fighting prowess, even if the crab was inclined to bluster." The voice was soft and fluid as a purr.

I cast about, but there was only Hime.

"The priest, in his eminent wisdom, provisioned you with *omiki,* which you applied to masterful effect." Incredulous, I watched her feline mouth shape words. "It is this one's humble estimation that master is adequately equipped for this undertaking, although perhaps —and I mean no disrespect— it would have been advantageous to have brought an extra fishcake or two."

"You can talk!" I blurted.

Hime regarded me with unblinking, golden eyes. "You have conversed with your father's spirit manifested upon a crab shell and consoled the yurei of your mother, and it is my speech you cannot credit?"

"B-but you're a cat!"

She gave her back to me, the twitch of her ear showing her affront.

"Hime-chan, I meant no discourtesy. I am only amazed. Why have you never spoken before?" But she would not relent, and I was left to apologize to her stiff tail.

She stalked upstream, leaving me to tag after. The morning passed in stilted silence. As the sun crested overhead, I fetched out my book of sutras in a bid to win her forbearance and flipped through it.

"How could priestly meditations help me defeat an oni?" I mused aloud.

Hime glanced over one white shoulder. "So now you have decided to heed the words of a mere cat?"

"Hime-chan, if I have offended you, then I am the basest of villains. We have been fast friends all my life, and assuredly you have my most earnest confidence and trust."

A tentative purr rose from her throat, but her tail remained implacable.

"Surely you are the wisest and cleverest of cats, and it is my sincerest desire that you help ease the burden of my loutish ignorance. Please, Hime-chan?"

Her tail relented. "Hannya-Shin-Kyo," she miaoed.

I paged to the appropriate sutra. "Meditation upon emptiness of form?"

"It is not merely the emptiness of your mind that it brings about, master. Does not *Kannushi* Akio say that to embrace the sutra, you must become it?"

"Yes, but I don't see—"

"Exactly." Hime sat so abruptly I almost trod on her tail.

"Why have you stopped?"

"Shh! The oni's cave is around that bend. I scent the old death of discarded bones, and his *youki,* his demon energy, prickles my whiskers."

I froze, my heart leaping in my chest.

"He breathes deep and slow," Hime whispered, "as a bear in torpor."

"Then now would be the time to strike. If I had a large stone or a tree branch, perhaps I could—"

Hime flattened her ears and hissed. "Are you in such haste to be devoured?"

"What? I—"

"If you truly trust me to look after your best interests, remove your clothes and give me your calligraphy brush."

As I was not at all in a hurry to be eaten or rent to bits, I did as Hime instructed, although more than a little abashed at finding myself unclad at the dictates of a cat. I hid my garments in the long grass and detached the *shide* streamers from my brush, cringing at each crackle and whish.

Hime bade me lay the book on the ground opened to Hannya-Shin-Kyo. Rising to her hind legs, she took the brush in her paws and used the stream's water to moisten my ink stone.

She wielded the calligraphy brush with dexterity, her claws and paw pads daintily manipulating the slender instrument. Starting at my feet, and referring often to the book, she painted the sutra on my skin. I kneeled and lay supine so she could continue decorating my flesh, shifting when she requested so she could paint my back. The brush whisked, damp and prickly, from the top of my scalp, including the ticklish curve of my ears, to the space between each toe.

"There," she said at last. "Your flesh has become Hannya-Shin-Kyo."

The novelty of the situation had eroded when I lay facedown in the dirt. "And how is this to benefit me against the oni?"

"You must discipline your mind to match your body, and you will be to the oni as the silence that frames a heartbeat, the stillness between thoughts, and the space outside the borders of the poet's composition."

"How do you know this?"

"I am a cat."

She said it as though it was all the answer I should require, and perhaps it was. After all, who was more adept than a cat at lurking unseen and gliding upon noiseless paws?

I composed myself, although the oni's proximity was not conducive to serenity, and strove to attain that elusive quietude where heart and mind embrace emptiness and the path of enlightenment becomes clear. I closed my eyes, pushing aside thoughts of the oni, my duty, and even the grit beneath my naked skin. I chanted the Hannya-Shin-Kyo and found a corner of tranquility.

"An estimable accomplishment, master," Hime said. "I can no longer see you. But linger a while. Horses approach."

I heard the jingle of leather and metal and the thut-thut of hooves.

"I must warn these travelers away from the oni's den," I murmured.

Hime did not reply.

"Hime-chan?" I stood, and she did not stir an ear tip, only continued to gaze at my previous posture.

Wonder would have sundered my tranquility, so I let it drift past, unmoved as the mountain by a breeze.

The horsemen drew closer, a trio of men. At their head rode a nobleman garbed in the elegant uniform of a military lord of high rank. The train of his ocean-blue brocade spilled off his horse's haunches. The silk was embroidered in white and silver threads with graceful butterflies identical to the ones that had adorned my mother's kimono—the Taira crest. *My* crest. The soldiers beside him wore simple gray, blazoned with the shogun crest of Minamoto no Yoritomo. Taira and Minamoto, implacable adversaries riding in accord?

I chased after as they cantered around the bend. In the side of the mountain, a black mouth dribbled water from a stony throat. The three men dismounted and tied their steeds away from the cave's entrance. The Taira nobleman strode forward.

"Oni!" he bellowed. "Rouse your lazy bones!" His voice bounced among the rocks, the echoes lingering.

A thunderous howl blasted from the darkness, and I clung to the nothing of Hannya-Shin-Kyo, setting each syllable like a shield against terror.

Out of the cave, a monstrous figure emerged, as tall as two men and massive as four. Its skin was the blue of smoke, and black horns sprouted from its head. A ragged tiger pelt draped its hips, and a gnarled, iron club, thick as my waist, hung from a ginger-striped thong.

"Who dares?" it roared.

The nobleman pulled a tawny jewel from his sleeve. It drank in the sun and cast off brilliant streamers of light. "Bow before me, demon, or feel the *gofu's* bite."

The oni crashed to its craggy knees and kowtowed.

I almost lost the rhythm of Hannya-Shin-Kyo then. The jewel, the *gofu*, was the pivot upon which my destiny revolved.

"Forgive me, master." The oni's voice was harsh, the grate of bone upon rock. "I forgot the cadence of your speech in the passage of seasons. What is your bidding?"

"Did you also forget the date? Tomorrow marks the end of our compact."

"I know the date." I felt the oni's words rumble through the hollows of my chest.

"And tomorrow will herald the beginning of a new one."

The oni snarled, baring a mouthful of jagged teeth. "No! You promised to free me."

The nobleman sneered. "So you may split my skull and devour me? I think not."

"I am oath-bound to exact no retribution upon you."

"I am not so foolish as to trust the pledge of a demon."

The hatred in the oni's eyes was as plain as it was tangible, hot as the blast from a furnace and black as deceit. "It seems that I am the fool to have credited the words of a traitor."

The nobleman brandished the jewel. "Malign me again, and I will set the *gofu* in burning coals and watch you writhe while your insides smolder."

"You may hold the key to my *youki*, Taira no Kimitake, but if you forswear your vow, the safeguards of our pact are forfeit. One day, I will rend the meat from your bones and feast upon your screams."

Kimitake laughed. "Empty words, barren threats. While I possess the *gofu*, you must serve me faithfully."

The oni spat. "With so much duplicity blighting your *ki,* how long do you think your good fortune will last? My patience is boundless."

"I, not the uncaring infinite, govern my fortune."

"Indeed."

"Enough of your insolence. I have decided that it is time again for my fortune to rise. The empire is tranquil, and so the emperor looks fondly upon Yoritomo. Therefore, I command you to upset this inopportune peace. Tomorrow you will raze the shrine below and slaughter all within it. While the countryside stews in turmoil, I will challenge and defeat you, and the emperor will set me as shogun in Yoritomo's place."

"You would defile a sacred place?"

"Of course not. But you would."

The oni glared in impotent fury as Kimitake and his escort withdrew.

As evening's cloak swept over the mountainside, Kimitake and his men organized a camp—raising a tent, gathering wood, and cooking rice. Kimitake retired while his soldiers paced the perimeter.

I crept into Kimitake's tent, secure in the protection of Hannya-Shin-Kyo, although I deemed it wise to wait until both guards' backs were turned and Kimitake's snores were loud and even before I scrambled in.

While I had expected to rifle through the sleeves and folds of his uniform, or perhaps upend boxes and baskets in search of a secreted compartment, the *gofu* was plain to see. Kimitake's outflung arm revealed a hand enveloped in a skein of white silk. Layer upon layer of fabric, sheer as a butterfly's wing, wrapped the *gofu* tight against his palm. By the wan flame of the single, burning lamp, it glowed through the bindings like a star.

Another item I had not provisioned myself with: a knife. But then, I had emptiness of form, better than any blade. I hoped. Murmuring my sutra, I began the onerous chore of unknotting and unwinding the silk. Before long, I knelt in a pool of air-light whiteness. But as I tugged the final strip, I felt sweat tickling my forehead. Without thinking, I rubbed it away. My fingers came back smeared with black, the Hannya-Shin-Kyo characters smudged from the droplet of perspiration.

Kimitake's eyes started open. We shared a moment of fright, then he flung himself away, gripping the *gofu* in both hands.

"Guards!" he shouted.

The two soldiers barreled in, knocking me to the ground. One thumped my head with his fist, while the other drew his *katana*.

"Wait!" Kimitake called.

The speeding *katana* stopped, its tip a child's fingertip from my throat.

"Before you die, thief, tell me who procured your services. Who knows about the *gofu* and the oni?"

"My service is not procured," I said.

Kimitake ignored my denial. "Tell me who spies upon me at Yoritomo's court. Give me the name of the man who dares plot against me, and your death will be quick. Otherwise, I will ensure that your last hours are a banquet of suffering."

"I am not from Yoritomo. My name is Taira no Chikazane. My father was Taira no Sukemori."

A sinister smile curved Kimitake's lips. "Sukemori's brat. You survived, after all. No matter. The detail of your death was only postponed."

He displayed the *gofu*, taunting me with the gem under my chin. "Be cheered, boy. You will die as your father did."

I stared at him. "*You* are the steel beneath the paper."

Kimitake swept from the tent, gesturing to his soldiers to bring me. He snatched up a burning brand while they hefted me like a sack of rice and dragged me to the black cave mouth.

"Oni!" Kimitake shouted. "Come out. I have a gift for you."

The ground shivered as the demon emerged. "What is this?" he grumbled.

"Do you not recognize him?" Kimitake said. "You devoured his father many years ago. I would have spitted him upon a *katana* as a babe, but now he shall meet the same fate as Sukemori."

"He is only a boy."

"He is old enough to die. Sukemori's death was too easy. You will eat his son alive, beginning at his feet." Kimitake flaunted the *gofu*, shoving it at the oni like a weapon. "Obey me!"

Hissing and yowling, a milk-white star detached itself from the abyss of sky and sped through the air. It struck Kimitake's outstretched hand, and the *gofu* flew out, an arc of gold. Four red stripes crossed Kimitake's wrist, possibly the first blood that Hime had ever drawn.

For a heartbeat, we hovered, frozen. Then the oni, Kimitake, his two soldiers, and I scrambled after the *gofu*.

The torch dropped, sputtering and dying on the ground, and all was blackness. Around me, the sound of frantic movement swelled the night, accompanied by the oni's bellows. A man screamed, and I heard silk and other, thicker things torn asunder. The chime of drawn steel rang out.

I crouched in the dark, searching. It was an impossible task. I would never find the tiny jewel before the oni turned its fury to me.

"Hime, I can't see it!" I shouted.

"Clarity!" she yowled. "Heed Akio's wisdom. This is another truth."

It seemed a questionable time to meditate, but I did as Hime advised. I inhaled and pushed aside the wet, ugly sounds erupting in the darkness, exhaled, and let my terror leave with my breath. I whispered the syllables of Hannya-Shin-Kyo and embraced the stillness between thoughts like a warm robe against the cold.

In the quietude of my mind's eye, I saw the sun. It floated upon the horizon in glorious brilliance, wreathed in garlands of fire.

I plucked it from the sky and opened my eyes.

In my hand, the *gofu* blazed, turning the clearing from night to noon. All activity stopped, fixated by the radiant jewel.

The oni gripped its iron club in a monstrous claw. At its feet, both of Kimitake's men sprawled in unnatural poses, their blood soaking the ground. Kimitake had drawn his *katana*.

"Oni, stop!" I shouted.

The demon regarded me. "I have no argument with you, son of Taira no Sukemori. Give me the *gofu,* and I will not trouble you."

"Do not believe him!" Kimitake shouted. "He is a demon and lies as easily as he breathes."

"As you do." I stepped forward. "Oni, lay down your club."

The oni did not obey, but only stood, watching me.

"Fool!" Kimitake cried. "You think possession gives you mastery over a demon's *youki*? It took me years to learn the secrets of the *gofu*. Give it back, or the oni will kill us both."

"I think he will not harm me while I hold it. Is that so, oni?"

The oni rumbled assent. "But know, young Taira, that though you hold my fetters, I will not volunteer the key. I will not willingly embrace slavery."

"That demon killed your father," Kimitake said.

"You may as soon blame my iron club for Sukemori's death," the oni growled. "I was your tool."

"Unbound, it will destroy indiscriminately. Demons have no honor, only hunger and lust."

I faced oni and kinsman. "The demon has shown more honor than you." I flung the *gofu* at the oni. Fast as thought, the oni snatched it from the air. He popped it into his gaping mouth and swallowed.

"Fool!" Kimitake shrilled. He slashed at me, a killing stroke, and the world slowed. For the third time that night, I watched my death approach. But again it was deflected, this time by the bluntness of iron.

"No," the oni said. "You have harmed this one enough." A claw snaked out, taloned lightning, and seized Kimitake around the waist. The club came down on the nobleman's head. A slight tap, but it rendered Kimitake senseless.

The oni bowed to me, the man clutched in his fist like a limp doll. "Your father was an honorable man too. You should know that his dying request was that I spare his wife and son. I was taken by his sincerity. I could not save your mother, but it was by my intervention that Kimitake's assassins did not find you. And it was my envoy, pledged to secrecy, who saw you safely to the priests' care."

"Envoy?"

"Here," Hime miaoed, twining herself about my ankles. "Have I not taken good care of you?"

"Wondrous good care." I kneeled to stroke her white fur. Purring, she sprang into my arms.

"Should I be concerned at the intricacies of your machinations, oni?" I asked.

The oni chuckled. "If I were younger, perhaps. But the spinning of the universe is long, and I have shed enough blood this turning of it. I wish nothing more than to meditate upon enlightenment and be left alone." He grinned at Kimitake. "But first, I will have a fine meal."

Hime and I made haste down the mountain, not wishing to be privy to the oni's vengeance.

We paused only to fish the stream by my mother's boulder, and so passed beneath the *torii's* gate well fed and bearing a bounty of fresh trout. I remembered to doff my *waraji* before I strode into the shrine, and I bowed low to Akio as he poured an offering of *omiki*.

"Welcome back, Taira no Chikazane-dono," he said.

"You must always call me Hiroki-kun, Sensei. All that I am, I owe to your teachings. After I have taken my priest's vows, I will explore my destiny with the name Oda no Chikazane to honor both my parents and this shrine. But to you, I will be Hiroki."

Akio smiled and bowed.

As was our habit, the next morning, Hime and I rose to greet the dawn. But though we watched the whirling surf until the sun gilded the waves, not a single crab came ashore.

TALE OF THE POET AND THE DOG

JAY LAKE

IT IS A TALE LITTLE told now, but the Fox women once climbed out of their heather beds and went to war. No one will speak of this behind the paper wall, and the farmers in their fields claim they have never heard of the story. Still, the rice men leave out their hopeful offerings of aburaage and politely look away when a *kitsune* slips past them.

Kamakura, Warring States, Tokugawa, even the Gaijin Shogunate—history does not matter to Fox women, any more than it matters to *kappa* or red ogres. They do not see our years, only the four seasons that turn in a wheel around the axle of the sun over and over again in eternal sameness. The islands are a cart to them, bound on a journey that never ends. To their eyes all men and their works are but rats in the rice bin.

Still, there was a time when a younger son in terror of the armies of Kublai Khan roused them from the bright country of their dreaming.

His name was Mimura. He had been trained in the gentlemanly arts of his day—poetry, painting, the proper arrangement of flowers. Being a practical lad he also knew how to dress a kill, bind a harvest and weave a bolt of cloth. Being a younger son, little care had been taken to prevent him from soiling himself with such base knowledge, and less care to school him to horse and armor and the discipline of fire and sword.

Mimura was in his father's audience chamber, attending the daimyo quietly from behind the ranks of the warriors as was his station, when the runner came from the *Chinzei Bugyo* with the red-and-white banners. A great hubbub arose, for many in Mimura's fathers lands had expected Lord Kifume to march from the north in the next turning of the seasons, but not yet.

"No, no," the messenger shouted, so bereft of his reason that he was beyond custom or duty. "The ships come, each with a hundred mounted warriors carrying bows that can shoot the shadow from the moon. The armies are gathering at the ports and beaches all through Kyushu. The *Bakufu* will have the west lined with steel to drive them off before they can land!"

"The shogun is a fool," Mimura's father said quietly.

With those words the entire audience chamber fell into a deathly silence. A man's head could be carried three times around the walls of Prince Koreyasu's palace for less, while his body was sent home in a tub of offal.

Mimura's father rose from his throne and drew his sword. "We will fight. It is our duty. But we will make a column of march on the Hill of Withered Plums, where we can watch the western sea and move great force to wherever the enemy will land. There are not enough men in all of Kyushu to wall the beaches as we have been commanded, but still we will prevail."

Mimura slipped away. This was work for oldest sons, *samurai*, bannermen and even hired swords from the *ronin* drinking in the villages. *He* was less than a servant. Mimura was also afraid, very afraid, but he wanted to see this thing for himself. A fleet of bowmen striding across the western waters would make such a mighty poem, if he grew old enough to command the words.

Though he could not stand and fight, he could sit and write, and so make a memory of them. So with an apology to the shrine in the forecourt, he packed rice balls and his calligraphy pens, took the oldest mule from the night soil man's wretched stable, clothed himself in rags from the ashpit, and set out west to see the sea before the steel marched forth in the hands of men.

Mimura sat in the empty doorway of a shepherd's hut east of Hakata Bay and watched the ships come from the water in their numbers. The Mongols were like locusts rising from the field. His father's men were arrayed in the fields behind Fukuoka Castle, formed next to Lord Kifume's army as it happened. The *Bakufu* had thrown over all feuds in defense of the island, and there was surely no different will in the palaces at Kyoto.

It did not matter who had been right about the disposition of the troops, his father or the prince. When the ships came the banners had rallied to meet them. And come they did, rank on rank of vessels riding the waves, until the waters were painted with wood and iron and the plaints of the Mongol horses on their decks were loud as thunder in the night.

He had a bit of a view, which he shared with a hard-bitten old dog and a great quantity of sheep dung. There had been a shrine here, but weather or hooligans had scattered its stones and torn the *shimenawa* rope. The dog whined softly amid its rough breathing, so he shared a rice ball with the poor beast.

"They will walk across the beach and slay my father and my brothers and all the men," Mimura told the dog.

The tail, bare with mange, thumped the dirt.

He tried to imagine an epic telling of what was to come, but celebrating the deaths of everyone he had known seemed beyond even the finest of the poet's art. A thousand Mongols could drown in every epigram, but not the wise and witty servants of his father's court, nor even his loutish brothers.

The first of the ships came to shore with a groaning of oars and the shouting of officers. In the light of the setting sun, the Mongol army began to find the beach, carrying the fall of Kyushu on the tips of its spears.

Mimura settled back into the shadows hut and prayed on what to do.

He startled awake in the night, unsure if he had been dreaming. There were fires on the beach. Drums beat, and even in the darkness Mimura could hear the creak of hulls. The dog wheezed like a forge bellows, as if the last of its life would be as great a struggle as its birth must have been.

In his small kit, he had brought an ink stone, three brushes, and a small sheaf of paper. Mimura spilled a bit of water from his sack and began to mix the ink.

He could not celebrate death, but he could celebrate what might have come.

There was no tea, there were no flowers, the shapes around him were unfortunate and infelicitous, but still he could find the words.

As summer takes the blossoms, he wrote.

That was wrong. Mimura meant to celebrate the coming victory, as if he could make the history of tomorrow true by writing it before the day came and thus force the world to follow his lead.

So the battle claims honor

"No!" Where were the words coming from?

The dog whined, turning its head toward him.

Cherries ripen and fall to dust

He threw down his pen. The dog hauled itself to its feet and stumbled over to sniff at the horsehair tip, still dripping with ink as it sat in the dust. It looked at Mimura and whined again.

"I apologize," he told the animal. "Perhaps you are someone wise, living out their life this way." He paused, and read the wretched poem aloud to the animal. Then: "Do you know better words for me?"

The dog shook its head, ears twitching. Mimura realized there was something wrong—had the ears stood up like that in the afternoon, when he'd first come here? And was that another tail?

Taking the brush in its mouth, the dog stepped lightly out of the hut, swishing both its tails.

Mimura felt a chill on his spine.

Not a dog. A fox.

Outside the east was becoming pale. The armies had settled, each a sleeping beast with ten thousand metal teeth. The Mongols and their horses, with their Korean and Chinese slaves, were arrayed upon the beach. His father and all the other lords of Kyushu were camped in the fields behind the castle, following the standard of the *Chinzei Bugyo* and the will of Prince Koreyasu.

Dawn would bring them to a clash of arms. He knew the Mongol arrows, their subject armies, their fierce hatreds, would cut down the armies of Kyushu as surely as the scythe cut oats in the field.

A faint rain rattled around him on the mouth of a breeze, though stars yet stood overhead. The fox bounded away, moving along the spine of the hill behind him and leaving the scene of the battle-to-come.

Though he knew well enough to hold a fearful respect for the *kitsune*, Mimura followed the spirit.

Dawn came with another pass of the cloudless rain, and Mimura was in a little dell lined with moss and ferns and beds of heather. A beautiful woman in a white kimono with the purple *obi* of a *daimyo* sat on a rock. He wasn't sure how he'd come here—the old fox had been running through the shadows of dawn, then they were here, without passing a door or gate.

"There are few guests in my house," she said.

He bowed deep. "It is my honor to present myself. I am Mimura, son of the lord at the Castle of White Mist."

She smiled, a small expression as filled with secrets as any ancient well. "You showed generosity to my husband when he was indulging his fancy of watching men at their play."

"He offered me no challenge, mistress, nor did he trouble me."

"Still you could have passed him by." Her smile flickered away like *koi* in a pond. "Have you come to watch the steel dance upon the sand?"

"No…" He tried to find words for what he wanted—that the Mongols would never have come, that the *daimyos* could fight and bicker as they always had, but life would go on in the villages and courtyards of Kyushu. This would be a burning such as they had never seen.

An old man, wrapped in ashy rags much as Mimura himself was, stepped out of the shadows of the heather. "Read her your poem, boy."

"Grandfather Fox," Mimura said, bowing again. "I am shamed by my poor words, and left them in the dust of the shepherd's hut."

"Wife, I tell you, he did not celebrate the sword, but wept for those who would fall."

The *kitsune* gave Mimura a long, steady look. "What manner of lord's son are you, not to pray for blood?"

"With peace we all keep our blood in our veins."

Her smile flickered back across her face, though she moved to hide it with a small hand. "You would deny the foxes and crows their feast after the fighting is done?"

"Lady." Mimura gathered his breath, his words, his courage. "These Mongols will not respect our ancestors. They will chop down the greatest trees, burn the heather dells, kick apart the shrines, and hang the priests up by their heels. The paddies will lie fallow and choked with mud, and the roads will be grown with weeds. There will be no Nihon to be home to red ogres and *kappa* and *kitsune* and all the other elders of field and forest. We will fall like the blossoms of spring and wither like autumn fruit. None will remain to honor you save ghosts and ashes."

"Honor." The old man hawked and spat. "Respect is rare enough, where is honor?"

"Husband," the *kitsune* said in a stern voice. Then, to Mimura: "Do you ask our help, who care nothing for the works of men?"

"No." He glanced at the spongy moss beneath his feet. "I ask your help, who care for the fields and forests of Kyushu."

"Hmm." She looked upward. "See, the sun is risen and yet it rains from a bright sky. It must be my wedding day come again."

"I—" he began, but his eyes were clouded with shadow and the swirl of a thousand fox tails.

The sun rose into angry clouds that closed in out of the last of night's shadows. They rode on a violent wind which snatched the fires from the Mongol's camp and spread them through the tents and horse lines. The storm wailed like an ogre that had lost its peach orchard. The Mongol ships strained at the anchors, chains and ropes threatening to part with the waves.

Mimura watched the banners of the *Chinzei Bugyo*'s forces rally under the storm's assault, his father's forces in the van. Then the rain closed in so hard he could see nothing except the pale whipping of mist carried on the rain, foxtails flying in the crest of the wind.

He sat in the doorway of the shepherd's hut as the rain washed history into the bay.

Later the old dog slunk in from the rain and shook itself off in the hut behind him. Mimura broken open his last rice ball and shared it with the Fox king. A single bare tail thumped twice on the floor. When the skies finally began to clear, Mimura bowed to his benefactor and picked his way down to the beach.

He had a tale to tell, though he knew the *kitsune* would never be more than a dream to anyone who heard his words.

Hibakusha Dreaming in the Shadowy Land of Death

Ken Scholes

Some of us started getting together for Group Psychotherapy after the war ended. I think it was Peach Boy's idea. He'd seen a flier, written in English, nailed to a post at the market and thought it might be a good way to practice the new language. He rallied up me, Golden Boy, One Inch Boy, and Urashima Taro, and we went down together to meet with the American psychiatrist, Amanda Fullbright Hampton, at her new office in a former Imperial Army officer's quarters in Tokyo.

We shuffled in each Tuesday with nothing better to do and sat in a circle, our hands wrapped around cups of steaming tea. Outside, American soldiers swaggered past Dr. Hampton's window, their pink faces shining and their white teeth flashing smiles. Each Tuesday, she made a great show of her annoyance and shut the blinds but I could tell she welcomed their looks. I found myself wondering if she didn't sometimes put on stockings and a shorter dress and high heeled shoes and go to the places where the soldiers drank in order to find one she could take home from time to time. Then, I wondered if maybe she might like to take me home sometime. Usually, I wondered this during our meetings. Apart from the fantasizing about Dr. Hampton, I found the Group Psychotherapy rather useless.

"What do you think about Kintaro's story?" Dr. Hampton asked me. She smiled and shifted her skirts.

I shrugged. "I'm sorry."

She leaned in and I tried not to look down her shirt. "He was talking about his mother."

I shrugged again. "We all know she was an ogress." When the psychiatrist frowned, I continued. "Well," I said, "she was."

The true nature of this was lost on her. She was looking for something underneath it, some kind of meaning. But we'd all learned the hard way that there wasn't any meaning left in the world. Most of the gods left a long while ago. Those who couldn't leave simply forgot who they were. Some of us who weren't quite gods didn't have that luxury. Of course, we couldn't tell her that.

Kintaro the Golden Boy cleared his voice. "Regardless," he said. "I saw a woman who could have been her twin down at the market and suddenly I felt—"

Issun-Boshi, the One Inch Boy interrupted. "You know who *I* saw the other day?"

"Who?" Momotaro the Peach Boy asked.

Kintaro looked stunned by the developing side conversation. He was used to getting more attention than the rest of us. He shifted his gaze from Peach Boy to One Inch Boy to me.

Dr. Hampton sighed. I started wondering if she were better in bed than she was at Group Psychotherapy and I was beginning to realize that she simply had to be.

I grinned at her and sipped my tea before turning to One Inch Boy. "Who did you see?"

"One of the Forty Seven," he said. Even Kintaro's eyebrows raised at this. Dr. Hampton tapped her pencil on her clipboard.

"I thought they were all dead by now," I said.

Peach Boy snorted. "That doesn't mean anything. Look at us. We're living proof of the Karmic Cycle." He grinned.

Only I wasn't so sure of this. Of course, I was also the only one of us who didn't know who he was.

Kintaro the Golden Boy remembered his past life as the heroic foster son of an Ogress. He could talk for days about wandering around with the regent warrior Minamoto no Yorimitsu and his Four Guardian Kings, fighting bandits and Spider Gods.

And Momotaro was quick to remind everyone that he distinctly recalled the smell and texture of the giant peach that he arrived in, and cried openly when he spoke of that childless old woman and her husband who found him, *Heaven's gift of a son* in his own words.

Next up was Urashima Taro, a fisherman who saved a turtle, visited the undersea Dragon's Palace and returned home to find that three hundred years had passed. "Imagine my surprise," he told us all that first day we met.

And there was Issun-Boshi, who insisted—despite his presently Sumo-sized self—that he spent part of his life in miniature because his own mother had wished to have a boy "even if he were only one inch tall." A skilled samurai, he killed an Oni with a sewing needle and won the heart of a princess who wished him to normal size...and then some, it seems.

Fact is, everyone knew themselves but me.

"And who are you?" Dr. Hampton asked me the same day she asked the rest of us.

"I'm hoping you can help me sort that out," I told her with a smile. She shifted uncomfortably and it was the first time I wondered what she might look like without her clothes. It was easier to think of that than it was to think of that unexpected and sudden end to the war, the piercing sunrise that swallowed two cities.

That was two years ago. Today, we were talking about our mothers (again) until One Inch Boy brought up the ronin and everything changed.

Kintaro leaned forward in his chair. "Where did you see him?"

One Inch Boy glanced at Dr. Hampton as if asking for permission to continue the digression. She said nothing. "At the G.I. Bar," he said, "on the water-side of the Dai-Ichi Seimei Building." He paused. "He'd been drinking sake for days." He paused again. "Well fed, too."

I knew the bar, down by Allied Command, but I'd never been there.

"Perhaps," Dr. Hampton said, "Kintaro would like to finish what he was saying?" She smiled; there was sweet sadness in it.

Momotaro stroked his thin mustache. "It sounds like he's done well for himself. I wonder what he's been up to?"

One Inch Boy shrugged. "I asked. He wouldn't say."

"Probably no good," Kintaro said. "Why, I wouldn't—"

But this time, Dr. Hampton did the interrupting. When she did, she uncrossed her legs and I saw a bit of creamy white calf. "Time's up," she said. "Please take a cookie with you when you go.

And we did, because like everyone, we were so hungry that even the Gaijin sweets appealed to us.

"I'm not sure about this," I told Peach Boy outside the bar.

"What's not to be sure about?" he said, smiling. "Maybe there's work to be had. Good money, easy money."

"But what about the Americans?"

One Inch Boy spoke up now. "Giving birth to a baby is easier than worrying about it."

I scowled. "What's that supposed to mean?"

Kintaro pushed past me. "Come on," he said. "It's fine."

We slipped in. There were uniformed soldiers everywhere, drinking and listening to loud music, talking even louder. I could smell their sweat. The four of us stopped and looked around the room. One Inch Boy pointed, then picked his away across the room to an old man at the far corner of the bar.

The ronin looked up at us and smiled, showing the gaps where many of his teeth had been. "Boys," he said, "it's good to see you."

He stank of sake and sweat and he wore cast-off American clothes. I thought I should recognize him but I did not, though the others did.

"What have you been up to?" Kintaro asked, clapping the old man on the back.

The old man chortled. "A little of this and a little of that. You?"

Golden Boy shrugged. "We're trying American Group Psychotherapy for free cookies, hot tea and English lessons."

"And the psychiatrist has shapely legs," I added.

"Well," he said, "I can drink to that." And he did.

One Inch Boy leaned towards him, lowering his voice. "You're doing very well for yourself. Are you working?"

The ronin flinched. "A bit," he said.

"We need work," Peach Boy said. "Maybe you can help us out."

The old man shook his head. "I don't think I can." He drained his sake and belched.

"And *I* don't think you work," Kintaro said. His eyes narrowed. "You drink too much to work."

The ronin shook his head and wagged a finger at the Golden Boy. "For my work, I drink just enough."

Kintaro still retained a great deal of his superhuman strength though he didn't look it. He'd traded the round, boyish features for the defeated look of a middle-aged man who'd watch his people rise and fall. But when his hand came down on the ronin's shoulder, I heard the old man's bones groan beneath the power of Kintaro's grip.

I pushed myself between them and scowled at Kintaro. "There's no need for this," I said.

Kintaro sneered. "He doesn't smell right." He looked around the bar. "He smells like *them.* Hell, he looks like *them.*"

I wondered if this was how it was meant to be now. Our gods had moved on. Only a few of us remained from those olden times and we lived quietly and wondered if the American bomb and boot might be the end of us. I wondered if perhaps waking up on the edge of that blasted ruin of a city was simply an illusion. Perhaps I was in Yomi, the land of the dead. And perhaps my companions were dead, too, and we were all wandering towards the edges of what might be life without ever truly finding it.

I put my hand on Kintaro's arm and brushed it off the old man. I was surprised at my own strength. "There is no need for this," I said again. Then I turned to the ronin. "I'm sorry for my friend," I told him.

He smiled but the light went out in his eyes. "Be sorry for all of us," he said with a quiet voice.

I looked at the others. All but Kintaro had looks of profound sadness on their faces. Kintaro still looked angry.

He spat on the floor. "Be sorry for yourself, old man," he said to the old man. Kintaro glared at the rest of us and stormed out of the bar. I noticed a few of the soldiers watching him as he went.

While Peach Boy and the others apologized for our friend, I slipped out behind him into a sullen, gray evening.

I caught up to him near the water. "Why are you so angry?"

Kintaro's voice was louder than was proper. "Why I am so angry? Why are you *not* angry? Look around you." He cast his arm about, encompassing the jeeps and soldiers moving freely among our people, freely upon our island. "We are hungry. Are they?" We are broken. Are they? And that old man—once a hero to his people—bends and takes every inch they'll give him. He's up to something. I know he is."

"But Kintaro," I said, "if we had prevailed would it be any different for them beneath *our* flag?" I swallowed, feeling myself tremble as memory washed me. "If we had their bomb wouldn't we have done the same?" Then, I let my voice become gentle. "Besides, each week we go to see the American Dr. Amanda Fullbright Hampton. We drink her tea and eat her cookies and speak her language. If the old man has found a way live in this hell who are we to judge him?"

His voice was sharp. "What do you know?"

And he was right. I knew little. I couldn't remember any of the war. Or anything before that. Nor any of my past incarnations. I woke up in a ditch on the edge of a blasted city, Peach Boy's tattered shoe prodding me. I woke up with no knowledge of myself, my skin nearly as pink as a Gaijin, my vision blurred, and my hair burned away. Within a week, my skin had darkened to its appropriate tone, I could see just fine and I needed a haircut. They said it was how they knew I was one of them after all.

By the time I opened my mouth to reply, Kintaro had walked away. It was the last time I saw him alive.

Kintaro the Golden Boy was killed the night before our next session with Dr. Hampton. We learned the news from the woman he rented a sleeping mat from in an Army warehouse that had been converted to sleeping quarters for low income workers.

"What happened?" Peach Boy asked her.

"He killed Americans. Fifteen of them."

"But why?" Issun-Boshi asked.

She shrugged. "Ask the old man."

We went to the bar but the old man was not there so we wandered about that part of the city, learning what we could without drawing too much attention to ourselves. Gradually we pieced together the end of Golden Boy.

Kintaro had stormed an American barracks with a katana and a rusty revolver he had found in a culvert. Some said he'd been shot over thirty times before he fell. Others said he'd not been shot at all. But many had seen the bodies pulled out from the building. The streets whispered the story to us but to my knowledge it was never reported in the American news. A thousand years of heroics and his last battle went unremembered by his foes, despite the price he extracted from them.

We still met at Dr. Hampton's office for our session. She pointed to the teapot and we served ourselves. "What would you like to talk about today?" she asked.

"Kintaro is dead," Issun-Boshi said. His voice sounded hollow to me and his eyes were red. "I would like to talk about that."

"Maybe we're all dead," I whispered. But no one heard me.

Dr. Hampton looked surprised and, for a moment, ambushed by our sudden honesty. Her eyes went wide for a moment, then she regained her composure. "What happened?"

We filled in the details as best we could. When we were finished, she let out her breath. "I'm sorry," she said. And suddenly, I realized she was crying and that there was greater beauty in her tears than there could ever be in her legs or breasts. For that hour, I did not wonder at all about how she was in bed. For that hour, her Group Psychotherapy was as mighty as old magic, as crafty as any dragon. She simply put down her clipboard and laughed with us, cried with us, as we talked about our fallen friend. As his story was told, her eyes became alive and her skin flushed, her breath caught easily in her throat. When we finished, she came around to each of us and hugged us. It felt improper even though her hair smelled as good as I had imagined it might and her body felt as warm.

"I'm afraid," she said as we stood to leave, "that this will be our last session together."

We looked at her blankly and Peach Boy spoke first. "What do you mean? We need you now more than ever."

She looked out the window and I realized that her face was not lined with sadness just from our loss but from some other loss inside of her. Then she recovered. "I don't think I can help you." She paused and chose her words carefully. "I'm not sure you need help." Then she paused again. "Besides," she said, "I have to return to America."

So one by one we filed out of her office, cookies clenched in our fists and stuffed into our pockets. Each stopped at the door and gave her a slight bow. She hugged each of us again.

I let the others go first. "I'll catch up," I told them.

I shifted on my feet before her, holding my hat in my hands. "I was wondering...." My eyes met hers for a brief second. They were blue with flecks of green in them and they were an ocean that could drown me. I lost my words and shifted again.

"Yes?"

I saw the curve of her breast beneath the white silk of her blouse. I followed the line of her neck to her tiny ears. "I was wondering now that I'm not your patient if you'd like to take me home with you sometime?"

She laughed and I felt the heat rise on my cheeks as I looked away. But her hand reached out and touched my arm and I knew then that her laugh was all nervousness and intoxication. She was drunk on the legend of us, or at least of my friends and their memories of Kintaro, and her smile told me her answer before she gave it. "I would like that very much," she said. "Meet me here at nine."

Bowing again, I fled into the rain to find my waiting friends.

We went back to the bar, hoping the old man would be there to tell us why Kintaro had attacked the Americans. His corner was empty so we took it and talked in low voices over cheap beer.

We talked about Kintaro for a while, then talked of the future.

"What will we do?" Issun-Boshi the One Inch Boy asked.

Momotaro the Peach Boy shrugged. "I have a cousin in America. He works in orchards in a desert near the Pacific. He's offered me work and will help me get on my feet there." He sipped his beer. "I think I will go there and start over again."

"You think they will let you go to America?" I asked. This sounded off to me.

He shrugged and grinned. "I am Momotaro. I will find a way."

One Inch Boy turned to me next. "What about you? Are you going to America, too?"

I shook my head. "I don't think so."

"Then what will you do?"

"It's hard to know what to do when you don't know who you are," I said.

"Me," Urashima Taro said, "I'm going back to the ocean." He saw our puzzled looks. "The here and now holds nothing for me. Perhaps the queen of the Dragon Palace will have me back." He sighed. "Otohime and her twenty maids in waiting. And this time, I'll let a thousand years pass before I return. And I will hope that our people—that all people—have learned a better way."

We raised our glasses and drank to that.

Peach Boy turned to One Inch Boy. "What about you?"

Issun-Boshi smiled. "I had a dream last night," he said, "of a monster rising from the waters. I think it would make a fine movie but I need to find a writer for it."

"Why don't you write it yourself?" I asked.

"I tried," he said.

And?"

"And," he said, "I think I'm better at being in stories than I am at writing them."

We all laughed, we all raised our glasses again, and we fell into silence for a while. Then, one by one my friends stood and filed out. I stayed because I didn't want to tell them I was going back to Dr. Hampton's in an hour.

The old ronin slipped in across from me as soon as they had gone. He was sober now and there was steel in his eyes. "It's not too late," he told me. "You can start over."

I stared at him blankly. His Gaijin clothing was gone now and he was dressed simply in black. His face was shaved, his hair combed. "What happened to Kintaro?" I asked him.

"It was never for Kintaro," he said. "But he asked. I should have kept silent. I should have found you."

I blinked. "What was never for Kintaro?"

He pulled a scrap of paper from his pocket and pushed it into my hands, then he folded his fingers over my hands and clenched them tightly. "*Amanonuhoko*," the ronin said and I remembered it.

It was called the Halberd of the Heavenly Marsh. It had made the world, or at least the beginnings of it. The memory jarred me after so long without recollection. A sea churned, an island formed. Creation.

The old ronin was speaking rapidly now. "I found it," he said. "My work. I've done terrible things." His eyes darted to the left and right. "They pay well for our artifacts," he said, "and I took their money like a whore and drank it away."

He withdrew his hands from mine and I looked down at the writing on the paper. It was a name and address in the United States, in a place called Michigan.

"I tried to tell Kintaro but he wouldn't listen. It had already been shipped. And even if it hadn't, he couldn't have used it. It wasn't for him."

Then he stood and turned to leave. My mouth opened and closed but I couldn't find the words. I had questions, but there were too many and I could not find the right one to ask.

Standing before me, he bowed deeply. "I beg your forgiveness, lord," he said. "I did not recognize you at first."

Then he left as quickly as he arrived.

When I tapped lightly on Dr. Hampton's office door, she opened it and ushered me inside quickly, looking up and down the street, her eyes moving with practiced precision.

She wore a shorter dress and silk stockings. Her bustline was tighter than the other dresses I had seen. It revealed the downward slope of her breasts, the secret shadow of her cleavage. Her brown hair was down now, covering her ears, and she did not smile at me.

Instead, taking my hand, she led me up a narrow flight of stairs and took me into her bedroom. She closed the door and turned down the lights.

I stood still, not knowing what to do. After two years of imagination and fantasy, the moment was upon me and I felt shame. A match flared and I saw her face in the glow of it. It bore resolve, not desire.

"I've watched you watching me," she said as she touched the match to the stub of a candle.

I didn't know what to say. "I'm sorry."

She turned around, pulling her hair up off her neck. "Unzip me?"

My hands shook as I worked the small zipper down. She waited there, the white horizontal line of her bra's back strap stark against her pale skin. When I saw that she wasn't moving, I reached up with my hands and parted her dress, pushing it over her shoulders as she released her hair and dropped her arms to her sides. The sleek fabric slid over her; I heard the sound of it rustling her skin before it fell crumpled to the floor.

Slowly, she turned and pressed herself against me. "Do you think this will help you?" Her right hand moved to the zipper of my trousers.

I swallowed and nodded.

"Do you want to know why I'm doing this?"

I nodded again.

She leaned forward and kissed me on the corner of my mouth. "All of your friends know who they are. In the midst of this death, they are alive." She kissed me again. "Maybe," she said, "if you feel alive you will know who you are."

I gasped at her hand's movement and another memory gripped me. Another beautiful woman in another time.

I felt something stirring but I did not know if it was life. She tugged at my clothing as she pulled me into her narrow bed and I let my mouth and hands wander her until we were both naked. Then, in the moment when I rolled onto her, fear seized me and I lunged out of the bed to extinguish the candle.

"What are you doing?" she asked. "What's wrong?"

But how could I tell her that suddenly I remembered another time, another lover, and knew that I dare not see her for who she truly was in this underworld we occupied? How did I tell her that if I saw her, like that lover long ago, she might haunt me all my days in the wrath of her own lifelessness?

Instead, I took her silently and in the dark.

When we finished, we lay close together and smoked American cigarettes. "I want to tell you the truth," she said.

"Yes?"

"It may hurt you."

I shrugged and smiled. "I've been hurt before."

"I think I am carrying Kintaro's baby," she said in a quiet voice.

"Oh," I said. I wasn't angry. I don't think I was even hurt by it. I may have even felt proud for my friend in that moment of revelation.

She continued. "I wasn't sure. I'm still not. But it *could* be his." She crushed out her cigarette. "I've decided I'm not a very good psychiatrist after all. I will go home and have my baby."

I wanted to tell her that I could come with her, that I could be a father to Kintaro's child—if it were indeed Kintaro's son—and raise him as my own. But when I opened my mouth to say the words, I felt a fist close over my heart.

"It was never for Kintaro," the old ronin said. I thought about the scrap of paper in my pocket and the address in Michigan where the Heavenly Halberd of the Marsh had been shipped.

I closed my mouth.

A match popped and she lit another cigarette, offering it to me. I took it and dragged on it, feeling the smoke fill my lungs.

"What are you thinking?" she asked me.

I leaned in and kissed her forehead. "I am thinking that you are a very good psychiatrist."

After she fell asleep, I dressed and slipped out into the night.

I felt differently, I realized, and it took me a moment to place the feeling. When it hit me, I smiled and wept at the same time because I knew it suddenly for what it was.

I felt alive.

Later that night, I went back to the bar but discovered it was closed. Military Police moved in and out of the building, barking orders, and I slipped back into the shadows and walked down to the waterfront.

I stood there for a long while, watching the water and wondering about Kintaro the Golden Boy, and Dr. Amanda Fullbright Hampton, and my other friends. I thought about the memories, just out of reach, that teased me now. Especially the memory of blinding heat and light, a wind of heaven that blasted down buildings and left only shadows to mark what had once been men.

The power of it forced me to sit.

I did not hear the man approach until he spoke to me.

"Good evening," he said in bad Japanese.

I looked up. Dirty light from the streetlamps painted a tall, slender American—middle-aged and wearing a trenchcoat and hat. "Good evening," I said in careful English as I stood.

He nodded towards bar down the street. "Bad business, that," he said. Soldiers were carrying a stretcher out draped in a bloodstained, white sheet.

"What happened?"

He pursed his lips. "An old man in the bar killed himself with a sword."

I was not surprised. "It is called *seppuku*," I told him. "I think you know it as *hara-kiri*."

The American nodded. "I think he recited a poem first. But I couldn't understand it."

Yes, I thought, he would do that. "It is the ritual to restore honor for a fallen or failed warrior."

"There are already too many deaths," he said. The man extended his hand to me and I took it. "My name is Ed Deming."

We shook hands. "I do not know my name or I would tell you."

He smiled and I saw sympathy in it. "These are hard times," he said.

"Yes."

"May I sit with you?"

I nodded and sat back down. He joined me. After a minute, I spoke. "You are not a soldier," I said.

Deming shook his head. "No. A statistician." My blank look conveyed my lack understanding. "I work with numbers," he said. "Probabilities and such."

"Ah. I see."

"I'm here to help with the census." Then as an afterthought, he added, "I'm from Iowa."

I looked at him. "Iowa?"

"It's part of the United States. Near the middle."

I pondered this for a moment. "Do you know of a place called Michigan?"

Deming smiled. "I know it. It's not far from Iowa. What about you? Are you from Tokyo?"

I shrugged. "I'm here now. I think I'm from Nagasaki. I'm—" I paused, trying to find the word "—I am *hibakusha*." It was a new word. *Explosion-affected person*.

A sadness washed the American's face. "I'm sorry," he said.

I shrugged again. "Nothing can be done for it."

"But you're okay? You're healthy?"

I nodded. "And my memory is coming back."

"Well, that's a blessing."

Perhaps, I thought. "So what do you think of our country?"

He smiled. "I think it's beautiful." And when he said it, I was reminded of the beauty in Dr. Hampton's tears when we first told her Kintaro had been killed, when she had joined us in our pain. Of course, I didn't know then that it had been her pain, too, because some part of her had loved Kintaro. "And," he continued, "I'm impressed with the resolve of your people to come back from this terrible, tragic war."

I snorted. "You think we will come back from this?"

"I really do."

I studied him now. There was confidence in his jaw line and the wrinkles in the corners of his eyes spoke of wisdom and humor. "What makes you think such a thing?"

"Because everything you've done so far, you've done all the way." His face lit up. "Think about it. If that tenacity were applied to being the best you could be, to providing the best quality of goods and services, you could have the world's wealth without firing a shot." His hands moved now as he talked and I felt something like hope growing inside of me. "If you have superior quality—both in your product and producers, your workforce and your managers—your productivity will climb and your expenses will fall. I really believe it."

"And you're a statistician?"

He nodded. "I am."

But in my heart, I knew he was a wizard, a sorcerer from old whose words were full of power and whose eyes were full of the future. I found myself wanting to believe him.

"How would we do such a thing?" I asked him.

He raised one finger, pointing it towards heaven as he extended it towards me. "First," he said, "transform the individual. That transformed individual will see himself differently, see the world in a new way. He will see the interdependency of it all and will bring about change." And in his next words, I *saw* the interdependency as he echoed the ronin's words. "It's never too late," Ed Deming said. "You can start over here."

We sat in silence for five minutes. Then I looked up at him. "I think you are a very wise man who will help my country very much," I told him.

He chuckled. "I don't know about that." He stood slowly and I heard his bones and joints creak. "But I do know it's late and I should be getting back." I stood, too, and when he bowed to me slightly, I returned the bow. Then we shook hands.

"I hope you remember who you are," Deming said.

"Thank you," I said. "I hope you enjoy your time in our country."

With a smile and a tip of his hat, the American Ed Deming turned and strolled away to leave me with my thoughts.

After he'd gone, I walked out onto the pier and found a place to sit in the deeper shadows. At some point, I fell asleep and I dreamed.

My people's automobiles were on every highway in the world. Japanese radios were in every home. Our goods went out from our tiny island and the wealth of the world came back to us. There were no more ronin riding their solitary wave, no more hibakusha with their souls burned to ash, and Nomi, that shadowy land of death, was a distant memory. Its gates were sundered and its captives free and alive again.

And I saw Ed Deming in my dream, speaking to my country's leaders, offering a new way to conquer and build our empire.

When I woke up, I knew who I was and I knew what I must do. I would go to America, to Michigan. I would take back what had been given to me so very long ago and I would climb once more to that bridge between heaven and earth, thrust the blade of *Amanonuhoko* deep into the sea and shake out its droplets over my land. I would recreate what I had created once before and the re-creation would drive out the shadows and spirits that had kept my people hungry and without hope.

I would do these things. But how?

"First," Deming's voice echoed inside of me, "transform the individual."

A declaration formed within me and I said the words to myself, silently. Then I spoke the words aloud to the empty night. "I am Izanagi," I said. "I will find a way."

And when I said it, I heard splashing in the water below and I opened my eyes. The moon had come out from behind the clouds and in its silver light, I saw my friend Urashima Taro on the back of an enormous, ancient turtle. He had two beautiful women with him and he grinned up at me.

"Have you decided yet what you will do?" he shouted.

"Yes," I told him. "Will your friend carry me to California?"

Urashima Taro bent in close to the turtle's great head and whispered something in its ear. He listened for a moment, winking at one of the pretty girls who giggled and blushed. "He says that he will carry you anywhere, Lord Izanagi, until you remember how to fly."

I bowed deeply to the old turtle and to my friend and his female companions. I stepped out of my broken shoes and peeled off my tattered socks. I removed my shirt and trousers, folded them, left them neatly on the pier.

Then laughing with joy and shaking with hope, I leaped into the cold waters of Tokyo Bay.

Lady Blade

JENN REESE

WHEN LADY KAGAMI FINALLY AWOKE, the first memory to brush her mind was that of her own death. She felt the blade slide into her flesh, remembered her surprise that with so little effort, her life had been ended. She saw the other women sitting in a circle around her, a similar wide-eyed look on their painted faces. She felt the braided cord crisscrossed around the hilt dig into the soft flesh of her hand, yet her fingers had maintained their grip long after the other muscles in her body had grown slack. She had fallen, softly and slowly—like a willow severed at its trunk—onto a pile of brocaded silk.

After that, only a deep sleep of bloody dreams strung together like pearls.

But now, as her sight became adjusted to the lantern light, she saw a man before her. Or perhaps he was simply a boy. He wore his hair in one long ponytail, slick and dark. The cut of his quilted coat and fitted pants seemed odd to her, and she didn't recognize the strange fabric with which they were made. She felt the man's hands wriggle underneath her, and they were warm. With little effort, he lifted her.

Stop, she said. *I do not know you.*

The man stumbled back, clearly surprised, but he did not drop her.

"My Lady," he breathed. "You... you *speak*."

Of course I speak, boy, she said. *Now release me before I call for my husband.* She had a husband? The awareness felt true, but brought little comfort for some reason. She hoped he was a kind man. Kindness was far more rare than goodness or honor, especially among men of war.

The man put her down gently. The stone upon which she was resting felt so cold compared to his arms.

"My Lady," the man said again, "I am sorry to tell you this, but your husband died long ago, in battle. He died a hero."

Yes, she thought. I knew this. *And I was at his side?* she asked the man.

The man nodded. "To the very end, Lady. And many legend-weavers and historians say it was you, not he, who won his battles."

Kagami laughed. *Ridiculous,* she said. *What am I, but a woman and a wife? I served my husband as I could, and did my best to honor him, but I am no warrior. You are mistaken.*

The man looked shocked again, and then thoughtful. "Lady, may I tell you a story? I haven't much time before I am discovered here, but the tale is important."

She could think of nowhere else she needed to be; nor, indeed, did she even know where she was. *You may,* she said, *but first, you must tell me your name and whether or not you mean me harm.*

He nodded once and said, "I am called Ryo, and I mean only to restore you to glory."

His answer confused her. What did she know of glory? But deep inside of her, something stirred. Something craved. Something remembered.

Tell your tale, she said, and waited.

The man—for she was seeing more man than boy now—sat on the dirt floor and leaned his back against the smooth wooden curve of the wall. He placed his lantern by his side. When he spoke, his voice was low and intimate, like a blanket of velvet on a starless night.

"Three hundred years ago, there came a dark time in our battle against the Horse King's armies, and our strength wavered. The Emperor had placed his faith in his twenty bravest generals, and although they were men of honor and courage, the number that rose against them was too great. For the first time in the Age of Emperors, defeat loomed near."

Kagami watched Ryo as he spoke, marveling at the shadows now settling across his face. He seemed older, wiser, sadder. Perhaps this was an act to lend gravity to his story, or perhaps he had truly seen more than his few years should have permitted. He made her curious, and curiosity made her feel alive.

"While the Emperor and his people prepared for surrender," Ryo continued, "twenty women took action. They were the mistresses and wives of those mighty generals, and although none had ever lifted a sword in battle, they swore to come to the aid of their lovers and their Empire."

But how? Kagami wanted to know. *How were these women to do anything but mourn for their lovers and slay their children when the time came?*

"Ah, there is the secret," Ryo said. He sat back, lifted his chin and closed his eyes, as if remembering something equally sad and beautiful. "Ancient magic, Lady. Ancient magic abounds in our world, if only one knows where to look. And if one is willing to pay the price."

Yes, Kagami thought. There is always a price. She felt phantom steel slide into her stomach, a memory so vivid, she could taste the blood that had pooled in her mouth and then cascaded over her lip in one long, elegant stream of warm rubies.

"And so they gathered," the man continued. "These twenty women gathered, though some were no more than girls. They gathered and fasted for a week, until their bodies were cleansed of impurities and their minds unburdened by the concerns of daily life. They cared no more for songbirds or poetry, for the latest fashions or the gossip of court. Then, and only then, were they prepared to perform the ancient ritual."

The ancient ritual, Kagami said. *Yes, yes.*

Ryo opened his eyes again and focused his gaze at her. "Each lady took up a sword, and each lady except one plunged that sword through her own body." He paused, but only for a moment. "The one whose courage failed fled and was never heard from again. Her husband died that very night on the battlefield, and neither is spoken of in any histories."

But what of the others? What of the nineteen?

"They gave themselves to their swords," Ryo said, his eyes aglow, his voice suffused with passion. "Their spirits joined with the swords that had ended their lives in the greatest of all magics, the spirit-bond. Servants carried these swords—some of them weeping the whole time, others screaming—across the Empire. They were delivered to the battlefields, and those nineteen ladies came to the aid of their lovers and their Empire. It is said that many of the generals cried out when received their bloody gifts, but none were refused. Those great warriors fought brilliantly. No enemy could harm them in battle. Within a year, victory was secured."

Ryo leaned closer to her. His warm breath puffed in the cold space between them. Kagami found herself frozen, transfixed. "The swords, my lady, are what won that most terrible war. The sacrifice of nineteen women. The bringing into being of the most glorious weapons of all time, and the most sought after: the legendary Lady Blades."

Kagami wanted to cry, but she had no tears. She had no eyes. She had no face. She had only the slimmest body of folded steel, ground sharp along one edge and fitted into a hilt at the base.

The memories returned, a flood of crimson screams and severed limbs. Of begging, of mercy forsaken, of unforgivable acts committed in darkness, and of death, death, death.

"My lady, you are so silent," the man said.

I am weeping, she replied, *in all the ways I can manage. I am weeping for what I have done and what I have become.*

Ryo stood and reached for her, his hand hovering above the flatness of her blade. He pulsed with life. Kagami yearned to taste his flesh, and the desire sickened her.

"But there is no cause for tears, great lady," he said. "You are revered and honored throughout time. You are *magnificent*." His body quivered as he spoke of her. She did not understand his awe. Yet... it was not unfamiliar.

She remembered men—first her husband, and then almost a dozen more. The memories were hazy at first, visions behind a parchment screen, lacking fullness. But as the memories resolved into color and scent and texture, she remembered more. She remembered each of her men, and her heart broke a little as she thought of their passing. Not one had fallen in battle, but death is cunning. Sickness, accidents, old age—against these enemies, Kagami was helpless. Her men had been good men, and they had all looked at her the same way as Ryo did now, their dark eyes glittering. They all told her she was beautiful and glorious, that she was like unto a god. And they all used her to kill.

But she had chosen this path, had she not? What person marries her spirit to a weapon and does not expect to fight?

Why are you here? she asked suddenly. *And where is here?*

Ryo's outstretched hand fell back to his side. "You are in a shrine, Lady. A place of honor. You were hidden here atop the

Mountain of a Hundred Owls three generations ago, so that you would be closer to the arms of the sky and farther from the hands of men."

Ieyasu, Kagami thought suddenly. She felt the ghostlike warmth of his body next to hers, saw his aging face and beard of white, felt the strength still evident in his arms, despite his many years and countless wounds. Ieyasu had wanted to protect her.

Despite this, you found me, she said to Ryo.

"Yes, Lady," he said, "though it has taken me many years and all of my money. My search has not been easy, but the rewards have been far greater than I expected."

She wished she could turn away from him, but she could not. Her gaze saw in all directions at once—the man, the wooden-slatted walls, the beams of the roof, the cold stone slab on which she rested.

I see no such rewards, she said coldly, and the man had the sense to hang his head and remain silent.

Eventually, he said, "Lady, I wish I could give you the time you need. I wish..." he searched for words, "...I did not have to do what I must do. But I was followed, and I haven't much time."

Do what you must, she said. *For when has it ever been otherwise?*

He reached for her then. If she'd had a heart, it would have stopped beating during that time, in that long expanse of moments when he lifted his arm and opened his hand and wrapped his fingers around her. She wondered then, would the braided cord around her hilt dig into his palm, as it had done to hers back on her last day as a woman? But it did not. Ryo's hand was girded in calluses. He was a man accustomed to a blade.

Kagami's spirit lifted, even as Ryo lifted her body. Joined with him now, she remembered not just the horrors of war, but also its brutal beauty. The way a warrior, trained in the art of fighting, danced more than moved… the way she became an extension of him, a partner bound in mind and duty.

"My Lady," Ryo whispered, "you are singing."

Kagami stopped. *I could not help myself,* she said.

"Nor should you ever." She felt his heart beating faster through the flesh of his hand. "It was beautiful."

A noise outside. And another.

You have lingered too long, she said. *They have found us.*

Ryo questioned nothing. Like a snake, he went from stillness to motion, smashing into the wooden door and plunging them both into the cold winter of the mountainside.

The men were waiting. Three in front of them and two circling around behind the shrine. Kagami saw them all in an instant. Without thinking, she told Ryo where they were. She knew which would strike first and she moved, slicing up, slicing across, blocking.

She never knew, after a fight, who had been in control: she or the man claiming to wield her. The answer was both; the answer was neither. With thoughts and words flashing between them faster than blades, they moved as liquid death. Only when she plunged through the heart of the last man did her conscious mind return and her thoughts once again travel in a line.

Ryo wiped the blood from her blade, his eyes glowing in the moonlight. He opened his mouth to speak, but said nothing. He shook his head slowly, clearly awed.

More are coming, Kagami said, and they were. She felt their feet on the mountain as they scrambled over rocks, heard the trees snort in disgust as the men sliced branches and cleared brush. *Many more.*

Slowly, Ryo returned to himself, though his breath still came in audible puffs to match the deep rise and fall of his chest. "There is an army after me, Lady. I am a condemned man."

How is this so? she asked, even as she urged him to start moving down the mountain. He headed for a trail of footsteps already carved into the snow's crust, the trail he had taken to find her.

"My story is nothing like yours, Lady. I will not waste your time with the telling of it."

You need say nothing more, Kagami said. And then, secretly, *For I can look for myself.*

In his mind, she traced the threads of his life. Woven with blacks and simple browns, his life was embroidered with reds in places, and also with pink flowers. The flowers were unexpected. She examined them more closely and saw a graceful young woman. Fair skinned with midnight hair, she laughed like chimes and danced like leaves on the wind. The ache of Ryo's heart suffused Kagami's spirit, and she wanted to weep for his loss.

But she is not dead, Kagami whispered. *If she lives, then there is hope.*

Ryo laughed, short and sharp. "You have hidden skills, Lady, but no. There is no hope. She is the Emperor's daughter, and sworn to another. Despite my service to the Emperor, the fact remains that my father was just a fisherman." He lifted a branch and slunk under it, keeping his feet to the foot holes he had made during his ascent.

Not 'just,' she said. *No one is ever 'just.'*

He nodded. "Even so, Lady, even so."

The lady loves you, Kagami said. *I can feel it still.*

Ryo stopped his trudging. Dark trees spread their leafless branches above them like a canopy of gnarled fingers. She heard his anguished cry though no sound issued from his lips. Kagami could barely remember love, but she had never forgotten sorrow.

Surely there is some way, she said. *We could slip into the palace and steal her away disguised as a boy…*

"No," Ryo said. "It's too late. My family is dead, and the Emperor has placed a price on my head for my transgression. I long only for revenge."

You lie, Kagami said. *I can feel you longing for more than that. I can taste your love like summer plums on my tongue.*

Ryo sighed. His shoulders fell, their tension released. "I mentioned a price, wondrous Lady. Ancient magic always has a price, and it has never, since time began, been payable with money."

Kagami thought on this and said, *Then what did you pay to find me*?

Around her, the crisp air distanced her from the world, from all things living. Only the warmth of Ryo's hand on her hilt connected her to the earth.

"It is different for each Lady Blade," Ryo said slowly. "The Lady Haruka does not allow her men to lie. The warrior in possession of the Lady Masako finds himself attending courtly functions and dancing until dawn. The Lady Tomoe will kill every dog unfortunate enough to bark in her presence."

Kagami was appalled. Had she issued such demands in the past? Did her men always wear blue, or worship the ocean, or kill their own fathers? She searched her mind and her men, and could think of nothing. She felt only fondness for them, and loyalty.

Ryo continued, "The Lady Blades are as different as their ladies, in power and in personality. It is *your* curse, Lady, that men fear most."

She was afraid to ask. She did not want to be petty, not after so many years.

Tell me.

Ryo smiled. If she were a woman, she would have felt his arms wrap around her shoulders and pull her close. "No man has ever touched your blade," he said, "and not fallen in love with you."

But, that is not so! Kagami cried. *I saw the Emperor's daughter in the tapestry of your heart. You are true to her.*

"No, I am not," Ryo said. "Even now, I can feel her memory fading. Even now, I wonder how I could have loved her, when a creature such as you exists in the world."

Kagami fell silent; she had no words.

Ryo laughed and began to pick his way down the mountain once again. Behind them, swords clattered against scabbards and men cursed, ever closer. But neither Ryo nor the Lady Kagami knew fear.

Eventually, she said, *Ryo, the price was too high.*

Smiling, Ryo said, "And that, my dearest Lady, is one of the many reasons why I love you."

In Fortune's Marketplace

Lisa Mantchev

In Fortune's Marketplace, our stall was a squat ugly mushroom in a flower-strewn meadow. No one who had a penny to spend wanted to know when they would die. They traded their silver for a golden stream of secrets, a cup of foamy pink love or a candy-striped stick of luck.

I cast my practice bones and watched with envy as a group of girls younger than I strolled past. In my smock, I was a cobweb to their kaleidoscope; a ghost, a shadow, a shade. I wanted to slip between them and disappear into the music and lantern-light. I wanted to watch the fireworks, get a taste of spicy food and freedom.

"Poor Kasei. Too bad you can't come with us. Too bad your dress is so old and your eyes so far apart." The Luckteller's apprentice, all in red, crossed her eyes and stuck her tongue out at me.

"It's not nice to tease her, Mieko." The Loveteller's apprentice shook her head. She didn't say anything more, but I could hear her thoughts twist between us.

So much bad luck, that one. No family, no honor. If not for the Deathteller, she would have starved in the streets.

I raised one of my bones and made as if to throw it at them. Mieko shrieked and grabbed the arms of her friends; together, they hurried into the whirl of the square.

A sharp blow between my shoulder blades reminded me I was always watched.

"With a girl so ugly, it's no wonder business is bad." Mother delivered another thump with her cane. She said a beating or two would be good for me: I was too much fire to her wood, and would burn her up if she wasn't careful. "Come inside and clean up this mess."

"No one wants to hear about death when they can go to the other Fortunetellers." I pocketed my practice bones and followed her inside, then started washing the mound of dirty dishes leaning tipsy against a wooden bucket. "They want to hear happy things, about their boy-friends and an unexpected but timely inheritance. So it's not my face's fault they don't come to you."

"Some customers want to hear about death," Mother said. Her knowing tone raised bumps on the flesh of my arms. "They want to hear exactly what the bones tell them. And they do not want to hear an impertinent girl speak when she should be silent."

I rinsed tea leaves from the bottom of a cracked cup as Mother settled herself on a heap of threadbare cushions that oozed stuffing from a dozen wounds.

"You, Kasei, are not bone of my bone. But I have taken you in. Fed you, clothed you. And when I die, all this—" she waved a hand over her moth-eaten kingdom like a beggar queen "—will be yours."

And when will that be? My cheeks flamed with rebellion; I didn't want her moldering tent or her visions of doom, but I didn't want to wait for them either.

Mother took my face in her hands and I braced myself for a slap that didn't come. "No Deathteller can see her own demise, Kasei. It is our blind spot, a place where Death can hide and we cannot see. A darkness too great for the brightest lamp of our Gift."

Some gift.

That time she did thump me, a ruby-ringed knuckle to the back of my head. I rubbed at the garnet pain and fought against tears.

"Too much fire, too much fire, she will not let herself cry. No water, no water, no water touches her flame," Mother singsonged before straightening abruptly. "Hand me the bones."

I fetched them, swallowing my angry words and a great lump of pride. A customer was coming. We would eat tonight: reason enough to make myself small, to be helpful and polite and please Mother.

They lifted the tent flap only a few minutes later. Grandfather Sato was crooked of knee and elbow, while Grandmother was all soft curves. They both bowed to Mother while I lit the candles and tried not to let my fire's curiosity betray me.

"Good day, Mother Deathteller."

"Esteemed Ones, for whom do I cast the bones today?" Mother held out her cup.

One of Grandfather Sato's gnarled hands dropped one coin, two, three, into the cup. "Our grandson, Taro."

Taro! I'd just seen him a week ago, eyes crinkled with laughter as he lifted a hand in greeting. On an errand for Mother, I hadn't a minute to spare, but I risked a beating for a shared fruit ice. I could taste sour cherry in the back of my throat as I looked at their twin expressions of sorrow and resignation. "Are you sure?" My fire spoke before I could stop myself.

Three faces turned in my direction, and the candles flickered in a gust of Mother's disapproval.

"We are certain, Kasei. We've been to the priest, and the Luckteller. This is... our final call." Grandmother Sato wiped her eyes with her sleeve.

I wanted to argue. I wanted to hit them with Mother's cane. *Leave! Don't ask her to look!* I wanted to shout at them both. I wanted to chase them away in a hail of broken tea cups, snap at their heels like a frenzied little dog all the way back to Cliff House. But the look Mother gave me promised a beating if I forgot myself again.

I lit the incense, closed the tent flap, and said nothing more to disgrace myself. Drum in hand, I squatted down next to her and tapped out the rhythm that would help her travel into the Gray Place.

Mother, satisfied I would behave, cupped the bones in her hands and began to croon to them. Her words tapped a path down my spine, stuck to me like sticky spider webs. I was only a step behind her and the incense became a mist that surrounded us both; I could barely make out her back as she strode to meet Him.

"Welcome, Mother." The voice was all around us; it resonated in my bones and turned my knees to jelly.

"Thank you, Most Venerable of all the Spirits." Mother inclined her head in the greatest gesture of respect I'd ever seen her perform. "I am here to ask about the death of the man-child Sato Taro." She cast the bones at Death's feet. Back at the tent, I heard the bones hit the dirt floor.

"Yes, he will die a few hours hence in a pool of blood. A violent death. The death of a warrior. Tell his grandparents to prepare themselves. They will need much strength in the coming days." His words flowed from Mother's mouth.

His grandmother cried out and collapsed against her husband; Mother rocked and crooned to the bones, and Death turned his eyes towards me.

I fell to my knees as his gaze bored a hole through my soul. The bones in my pocket jumped with my first vision: I saw the flesh fall from Mother's bones, her eyes dim, and her lifespark sputter. I saw myself, ensconced in her tent, holding her cane, wearing her ring. I was the Deathteller.

Then Death reached out to touch a finger to my forehead.

"No!" I screamed, jumping away from Mother, away from Death. I stumbled through the bones and ran from the tent, gasping for air and eyes streaming tears. I ran, with Mother's voice chasing me. I ran, with the promise of Taro's blood shining under my fingernails. I ran from the marketplace and into the night, with only one thought.

I have to get to Taro.

I was like a creature possessed, afraid to look over my shoulder in case Death gave chase through the streets. He might have followed me to mete out punishment for my disobedience, but I wasn't stopping to check.

My practice bones rattled in my pocket, and the clackety-clack picked at my skin and my hair. I could hear them now, the bones, as I skirted the noise and the color of the central market. Their voice oozed from the Gray Place and wound through my head—

Kasei, why are you running, Kasei? The Mother, she will be angry! And Death… Death will not be pleased….

Along a crooked alley—

We know things, great things, terrible things. We will share them with you!

When I passed the apprentices now dancing with the village boys—

That bold Mieko, she'll die in childbirth, and her child too, whispered the horrible bones.

I clapped my hand over my pocket to silence them, but they roiled and tumbled under my palm. I could feel Mieko as she shuddered and writhed; blood streaked her thighs and her belly heaved, then stilled.

"No!" I whirled around, sought the safety and solace of a shadowed alleyway. An elderly woman dozed in a doorway—

She'll be as cold as the stones by the morning! the bones chittered and cackled. They exhaled a frost that seeped outward and grasped at my fingers.

Never had they spoken to me so in all the time I'd spent with Mother. She'd thought me stupid when I couldn't coax even the simplest prophecy from their marrow-middles, thumped me with her cane for being unable to say when a wasting cat would cross to the other side. I'd prayed then for the voices to come, to whisper in my ear.

Now I wished for nothing but silence. And a way to save Taro.

Taro! The Master has touched him—

"Enough! I won't listen to you any more!"

I hurtled myself out of the maze and to the river's edge. The banks were empty tonight, but the memory of a thousand leashed birds tangled with the silver scales of sweetfish and floated over the surface of the water.

I drove my hand in my pocket and ripped my skirt nearly in two as I grabbed at the bones. They tumbled this way and that, snapped and snarled with the memory of jaws and teeth.

No, Kasei, we are bone of your bone!

I flung them into the water before they could say more. For a moment I thought my fingers had gone with them, so empty did my hands feel, but no, my fists shook at my sides, full of fury and panic. My breath came in short pants that sparkled in the night air. The bones bobbed for a moment, then sank beneath the black surface.

"I won't be the Deathteller," I whispered. "I won't!"

The bones laughed at me as they found each other in the current. Buoyed by the waves and embraced by the water, a ragged bit of lower jaw kissed the skull as vertebrae slid into place. Four spindly legs discovered their paws as the creature paddled to shore. It shook the river-damp from its ribs and leered at me through empty eye sockets.

"What are you?" I took a step back.

Kasei doesn't know us when we aren't in her pocket. Maybe if we get a bit closer—

It grinned; lantern light stained its fangs red and yellow.

"You cannot be my practice bones." I wished myself any place but this one. "Mother would never give me a spirit animal in its entirety. That's forbidden to apprentices."

The creature's sides heaved in silent laughter.

Mother didn't know. We crept from her box, from her bed, from her tricksy bag tied up in silk. You could not hear us speak with our jaw under her bed. You could not scratch behind our ears with our skull under her pillow. So out we came when she looked the other way. To whisper, whisper secrets in your ear.

I shuddered at the idea of those teeth against my ear. "I won't listen. You're a demon come from the Gray Place to plague me. He sent you to bring me back."

The diminutive framework chastised me with a shake of its head. *We can tell you about your Taro.*

"Liar." I wanted to run, but what if the bones knew a way to save him?

The bones cannot lie. The skull tilted to one side and winked, if that were possible.

"I know you can stretch the truth, if it suits you." The space between us dwindled, but curiosity anchored me. Could they really help me help Taro? "What are you? If it's not rude to ask—"

The animal rubbed against my ankles, tailbones twitching.

Head of a fox, tail of a raccoon. A few other bits borrowed from here and there. Now if you would be so kind?

The bones vibrated in a cadaverous purr as I touched a hesitant hand to its back.

Right there, just behind the ear—

"You… don't have an ear." I recoiled a bit at the thought, then made a guess as to where the spirit creature's ears would be.

The fox-thing lolled against my hand, its back arched with bliss.

"Now tell me how to save Taro, *kitsune*." For surely this must be a trickster, a malevolent fox-spirit sent to lure me back into the arms of Death.

The beast hissed at me; where the lower jaw met the skull, a star ball glowed with silver light. "Stupid girl! A true *kitsune* would not bear the tail of a raccoon. One tail, five or nine; they would be fox tails. And I would have fur of purest gold! My ribs would not show." The creature hissed once more for good measure and stomped a few feet away. "Perhaps this girl doesn't want Jiaonuo's help. Perhaps she'd like to let her Taro die…"

"I'm sorry, forgive me." I gave chase, dropped to my knees in the path before the skeleton-fox and made my very lowest bow. "Please, Jiaonuo, forgive a stupid girl."

"We forgive you, bone of our bone, even though you are the rudest girl we have ever known." Jiaonuo nipped the end of my nose and then turned, tail twitching. "We shall take you to Taro. And perhaps, if you are good, we shall help you save him."

—

Bits of twig and foliage leapt from either side of the path as we walked. Within a few minutes, Jiaonuo wore a coat of summer debris: rice chaff and leaf mold in stripes of white and black. Her tail, that sad raccoon's tail, dragged limp through the dirt behind her.

It's not worth the effort to hold it up, the bones said with a sniff.

Moonlight leeched the color from the Fortunetellers' vacant tents and bedraggled banners. The dancers were gone, tossed by the wind like discarded sweet wrappers and broken porcelain cups, their fortunes dissolved like brown sugar cake on the tongue.

They think it a game. Jiaonuo sniffed a torn golden ribbon that leaked secrets into the mud. *This one—*

I clapped my hands to each side of my head. "No, I want you to promise me. No more deathtelling tonight. Please, venerable spirit. We must get to Taro."

Jiaonuo tilted her little fox-head to one side and then nodded. *Because you asked nicely. Now if we are to save your little friend, we must get to his house.*

"I know the way."

Take your fingers out of your ears, idiot girl. There are better ways for me to get in your head.

Her toenails went clackety-clack on the stones underfoot as we tiptoed through the main square and past the permanent storefronts. The thatched roofs of lesser dwellings.

"Where is everyone?" I'd been out at night before, and even in the dead of winter there was activity in the town. Deliveries to make and wares to restock: crates of pears trailing a mysterious perfume or highest quality paper to fold into tiny flapping cranes. Grass mats to sweep and babies to shush and the slams of sliding doors. But now there was nothing and no one. Just me, and the fox spirit, and a tiny, teasing wind that chased us down the road to Cliff House.

I hesitated at the bamboo gate, but when Jiaonuo marched past me, I hurried after her, through the water garden and to a sliding door cracked to let in scent of night-blooming jasmine and prickly water lily. Jiaonuo nosed the door aside and disappeared into the cool blue interior of the house.

I kept expecting someone to stop us. Surely his Grandmother would be keeping a vigil at his side now that the Deathteller had consulted the bones and made her pronouncement? But no one was there. The lanterns lay cold and overturned. Dry leaves danced across the floor, twigs lay snapped underfoot. When the moon disappeared, I froze. Jiaonuo opened her mouth, and the silver ball of light at the back of her throat guided us to the very end of the hall.

Taro lay on a braided grass mat, a thin blanket drawn up to his chin. In the silver light from her mouth, he looked frost-bitten, frozen in place. I dropped to my knees beside him.

"We're too late." His hand was so cold—

Jiaonuo sniffed his blanket, his pillow, finally his mouth. *No. But the sleep is a deep one. Someone is trying to stop us.*

The screens on the far wall slid open with a series of thumps, and a wide wail of screaming wind rushed in. Black streamers of my hair whipped me in the face as I tried to pull Taro back the way we'd come. "He's too heavy. I can't lift him!"

Mother stepped into the breech, flanked on either side by Taro's grandparents. They swayed, glassy-eyed. Their limbs moved like puppets on limp strings.

The Deathteller lifted her hand and pointed a finger-bone at me. "Impudent child. Do you know what you've done?" She included Jiaonuo in her glare. "And you, you wretched carcass, you shivering skeleton. How dare you?"

The fox-spirit hissed and arched her back. "Where is my tail, crone?"

Taro's grandparents jerked on their invisible lines as Mother laughed. "You'll never get it back now."

Jiaonuo's jaw unhinged in a cry that filled the room and poured into my ears. Bones rattled and fell to the floor; the star ball exploded toward me. Bits of light crawled under my fingernails and scrabbled through my breasts. Jumping to my feet, I let Taro slump against the wall as I scratched at my skin and tore at my clothes. The pain tapped through me, clackety-clack. I looked at the world through a fox's eyes, smelled Mother's fear through a fox's nose.

Jiaonuo held out my hand. The bones leapt to her call, swirling in a vortex of silver starlight above my palm, all winking sharp corners of tooth and nail. "I will carve the flesh from your face, and enjoy every rivulet of blood and chunk of skin," she said through my mouth, "unless you employ that useless wad of matter between your ears and get out."

"This isn't over, dark sister." Mother leapt into the night sky, robes trailing over the moon before she disappeared. Taro's grandparents fell to the mats.

Skin still crawling with starlight, I knelt next to him. "Taro?"

"Kasei?" It was nearly a man's voice; the deep timbre of it startled me.

"Yes, it's me. Get up. We must get you out of here."

His grandmother lifted her face from the mats, reached out a trembling hand. "My dear boy, don't leave me—"

"We have to go." Jiaonuo helped me jerk Taro to his feet and drag him down the hall.

"Where are we going?" His voice sang in my chest, and Jiaonuo purred.

That's enough of that, I growled at her. *And just as soon as we get him out of here, you are evicted from my body.*

The fox's laughter bounced between my ears. *I told you I had better ways of getting in your head.*

The bones in my pocket rattled in a dry, listless rhythm as I coaxed Taro into the trees behind Cliff House. As full as my head was with my unwelcome guest, I couldn't help feeling very alone without their familiar clackety-clack.

Don't be stupid. I'm right here, Jiaonuo said with a sniff.

That's the trouble, I retorted. *I'd prefer you were in your own bones and back in my pocket where you belong.*

"Please let me rest," Taro said, startling everyone. "I have to sit down."

"You can sit when we're safe." Jiaonuo and I put our shoulder more firmly under his armpit and dragged him a few more steps.

Safe from Death? I ventured.

It sounds more comforting than "Perhaps we should not wait here for the Deathteller to find us", yes?

I didn't know if there existed a place far enough that we could run from the Deathteller's prophecy. Taro was to die very soon, a violent, warrior's death she'd said, but the figure that struggled alongside me was hardly strong enough to lift his own feet, much less a sword.

This is the trouble when an apprentice dabbles.

I glared inward. *And whose fault is that, exactly? I never would have followed Mother into the Gray Place if you hadn't collected your bones and started whispering to me.*

Jiaonuo didn't answer. Instead, she withdrew her strength from my arm, and I was forced to deposit Taro on the nearest rock.

He cradled his head in his hands as the moonlight sidled through the trees and painted his hair with blue ink. "My head pounds like the drums. Why did you bring me here, Kasei?"

I stood, uncertain. "You were in danger. Do you remember what happened before you went to sleep?"

He lifted his head with effort and gave me his lopsided grin. "I went to the market, ate some sweet cakes and drank a glass of rice wine—"

"Danced with the apprentice Fortunetellers," I finished for him, and Jiaonuo sniffed with disapproval.

"Maybe one or two," he conceded. "I would have danced with you, if you'd been there."

That tied my tongue into a knot. Jiaonuo danced with impatience as I sorted through a tumble jumble of emotions: while my insides turned to eel jelly, fear still ruled over all else.

"And after the dancing?" I finally managed.

"I went home. My grandmother made me a cup of tea and scolded me for staying out in the night air. She seemed upset about something, but I was too tired to ask what."

"And the tea?"

He thought back to the cup. "Bitter, and so green I could smell the grass growing."

A sleeping draught then, one of Mother's concoctions designed to help the death-fated ease their transition to the Gray Place. But laced with something else, or his head would not be pounding so. Something to ensure the Deathteller's prophecy would be fulfilled.

Mother was afraid, then, and trying to help Taro the way a butcher helps the hog to slaughter.

"What's happening, Kasei? Tell me."

He was the only boy who'd dared venture to the Deathteller's tent, the only one who would toss me the ball on the courtyard, the only one whom I thought looked nice when he smiled. How was I to tell him that Death waited for him? How was I to tell him to fight, to run, to take me with him? "The Deathteller named you. I was there when she cast the bones."

I felt him stiffen with surprise; the space between us spasmed. "When?"

"An hour. Maybe less."

"That's all?" When I nodded, he jumped to his feet. "How?"

I lowered my eyes, burned by his gaze. "I don't know exactly. But He promised bloodshed. A warrior's death."

"I have to get back to Cliff House. I don't even have my sword—"

I couldn't have moved myself, but Jiaonuo knelt next to Taro and put my hand on his arm. "You will not die. I promise you," she said through my mouth.

He stared at us with changed eyes; I thought for certain he would see her inside me. "You look different here. I never noticed the light in your eyes before." He brushed my hair back over my ear.

Jiaonuo laughed with my mouth and I struggled to take back my words from the fox-spirit, but couldn't manage it. "The bones have changed me. I am not as I was."

"And what are you?" he breathed.

"Yours," we both said.

The kiss we shared was sweeter than plum candy, and lasted twice as long. He sidled into my head alongside the fox-spirit, the Deathteller, the vision, the rattling bones, and crowded all else out.

I dragged myself from his lips. "We have to go. I must get you away from here."

"We cannot run, Kasei. I won't dishonor my family that way." Taro stood. Through the trees, Cliff House bathed in a puddle of quicksilver. His grandmother's wail parted the leaves; wind shredded the paper screens and tore chunks from the walls. "Do you see? Death is taking his vengeance already."

I spat on the ground at his feet. "That for Death."

He turned and seized my wrist, jerked me to my feet. "You say it is my destiny to die. Just as it is your destiny to become the Deathteller. You cannot gainsay the fortune once it is said."

"I did not read that fortune. It was never my own!"

"We cannot help that now." He turned and towed me through the trees; I dragged my heels, twisted and pulled. I scratched at his hands, bit down upon his ankle and kicked him with all the strength I could muster.

Help me stop him Jiaonuo, please!

She didn't answer, but Taro had words enough for them both.

"And what would happen if the prophecies of the Fortune marketplace no longer came true? Luck and love and secrets trampled underfoot, given no more heed than a lisping child telling lies?" He stopped long enough to shake me. "Is that what you want? To see everything that we have been, everything that we are crumble to dust?"

There it was: the strength to pull free from him. It blazed up inside me with all the fire of Jiaonuo's lost nine-tails. "The bones of my bones are mine, to do with as I will!" I scrabbled at my chest with my fingernails. Jiaonuo howled in my head and tried to claw her way back to the innermost part of me, but I caught her between my fingertips and wrested her kitsune-soul from me. The bones scattered in semi-circle, but still I blazed. Every tendril of hair crackled, and my skin burned with fox-spirit magic.

I turned to Taro just as Death found him with His sword. "No!"

An arc of blood spattered my face and arm. Even the moon dripped with gore.

Mother stood behind me, whispering in my ear. "He will die, he will die a few hours hence in a pool of blood. A violent death. The death of a warrior." Her bones rattled in my ears.

"Cliff House will endure. The marketplace will continue. And life will go on, little Kasei."

Taro fell to his knees; his smile was quiet and entirely for me.

"Yes, it will." I turned to Mother. "But not for you. I have seen *your* Death."

She paled and took a step back. "No! I won't listen."

"I do not need your ears to make you hear." I pushed into her head. "The flesh falls from your bones, your eyes dim, and your lifespark sputters."

With her screams, she tried to silence my voice out before I could say the words. But I tore the cane from her hand and broke it across my knee. "You have foretold your last fortune. I am fire to your wood."

She shriveled under my gaze, under my hands. A silent scream poured from her mouth, but found no listening ear. I killed her then, burning her with all the magic left in me, and it was as I said it would be. All that remained—her ruby ring—landed on the pile of ash with a thump.

Jiaonuo's bones skittered closer, whining with incoherent happiness. *My tail!*

"That's just her ring." I staggered to Taro's body and pulled his head into my lap. His blood painted my fingernails again, but this time it was real.

"Stupid girl, that's just what it looks like." Jiaonuo scooped the ring up where her mouth should be. The fox-spirit gave a great heave, as if she'd swallowed the ocean. The ring collided with the star ball in the back of her throat-place, its silver light flickering, exploding outward, then settling in silver skin on the bone of my bones.

Then Fortune stared down Death. "You owe me a boon, for giving my tail to that harridan."

"It was good for you." Death sniffed at Fortune's human form. "How else were you going to learn some humility?"

"Nevertheless, I would be a most grateful Spirit if you'd restore the boy."

"And the girl?"

Fortune reached out, touched a finger to my forehead. "I claim her, as do you." She slid the ruby ring over the middle finger of my right hand. "She is your Deathteller, and my Lifegiver."

Death grumbled and took her by the elbow. "That's too many titles for one so young and silly."

Fortune laughed and kissed his hollow cheek. "Perhaps yes, perhaps no. That's for her to decide. Now return the boy, and let's get something hot to drink."

They left on a southerly wind, and Taro opened his eyes. He touched a finger to my lips. "Your face looks as it should."

"And you are almost more trouble than you are worth, Sato Taro." I sniffed back my tears; Deathtellers don't cry.

"Why did you bring me back then?"

My only answer was a kiss.

A TROLL ON A MOUNTAIN WITH A GIRL

STEVE BERMAN

RESOLUTE, OWEN CASHED OUT HIS 401K—at a penalty—and set out on his world-spanning tour to be eaten by a monster. He packed two brand-new suitcases: one with comfortable clothes, the other with library books. His plan was to study the books on route and, at each destination, whether English countryside or Nerluc in Provence, to unpack a shirt, pair of slacks, and clean white boxers, and meet his fate looking fresh and neat.

But by the time he had reached F in his notebook—*Fachen-Orkney Islands*—undevoured, Owen had had to make some adjustments, such as washing clothes in hotel sinks with tiny bottles of complimentary shampoo. He could not bring himself to meet death appearing too disheveled.

He went from Europe to Africa, then back to New Jersey—he knew the rational thing would have been to search the Pine Barrens first, being they were an hour away when he began his tour, but the thought of breaking alphabetical order paralyzed him. Finding nothing lurking or skulking anywhere, he grew concerned.

Even Tokyo was turning out to be a disappointment The English language notebooks were rapturous about cherry blossoms and neon. None mentioned an ancient hag's lair on *Nabekura-yama.* The small town of Tōnō was no better; no one knew her story. Didn't local monsters deserve some press? Even Leicestershire's tour books mentioned the threat of the Black Annis. Not that Owen had lucked upon her.

Waiting for breakfast, Owen paged through the yellowed book of folklore, the sole surviving text he had brought from New Jersey. The rest of Owen's books had been abandoned in hotel rooms around the globe. He sometimes wondered if any of the maids had an interest in the echidna or the tarasque.

Owen always treated himself to a large breakfast before setting out for the hoped-for monster's lair. Back when he worked as an accountant, he had allowed his workplace frugality to bleed over to his home life. Mornings were two cups of instant coffee with artificial sweetener and a piece of rye toast. Originally, he'd thought it an exercise in clever discipline to have a sandwich for lunch that began with the day's letter: Monday was a melt sandwich, tuna, which he could have chosen for the next day but that was always toasted cheese (it was unfortunate that no weekday began with G or C). Wednesday was a wrapped leftover in pita; Thursday more toasted; and Friday he was free to lunch out as long as he did not spend more than 7.00 pre-tax and –tip.

But now, Owen saw no reason not to spoil himself. Every meal might be his last. So he indulged in local dishes, ate things like beans and black pudding or *prima colazione.*

The Tōnō hotel's restaurant was quiet, the waitresses busying themselves folding napkins. Owen sat waiting for plates of grilled fish, rolled omelet, and pickles, with rice, of course. He sipped hot tea, unsweetened; he did not know how to ask for sugar in Japanese and there was none on the table.

"Excuse me, but are you American?"

Owen looked up. The man standing by his table's empty chair looked to be in his late twenties but a good shave and haircut might have lost him a few years. He wore an open, wrinkled button-down shirt, the pale t-shirt beneath even more creased. The knees of his jeans were threadbare.

Owen nodded. "Though some would say New Jersey doesn't deserve to be a state." The joke was more for his own benefit. He was uncomfortable with the unexpected.

The guy smiled and unslung an immense backpack he had been carrying. "Great. Would you mind if I joined you? I've missed English."

Owen sat up straighter and lifted a hand towards the empty seat.

"I'm Saul."

"Vacationing student?"

Saul laughed. Owen noticed very large teeth, the bottom set chipped and askew. "Half right. I'll be a teacher, or will be next week in Moriokashi. Thought I'd do a bit of roughing it before I start."

A silent waitress brought over Owen's food and took Saul's order with a nod.

"Have you been to Mt. Nabekura yet?" Owen hesitated to take his chopsticks to the meal. Which to eat first? He couldn't discern what sort of fish it was, so that left it to F. Omelettes should be eaten next, but they were mostly eggs, so that took precedence. But then pickles were really cucumbers....

"I may go tomorrow. I just want a couple nights indoors on a soft bed."

During the past month, Owen had kept his quest secret. But now, almost at the end, he needed to tell someone, if only to reinforce his hope that today would be his last. So he leaned forward and whispered, "I've been hunting monsters."

Owen was reasonable. He blamed his mother for only half his fascination with men and monsters. As a child, he spent every weekend with her on the plastic-sleeved sofa in the den. They would each take handfuls of salty popcorn from a big metallic mixing bowl and watch whatever old horror movie was on the UHF station. His father had spent every weekend at the shore, working on his boat, no matter what the season. By the time Owen was old enough to cook the popcorn on the stove by himself, he realized why men name their boats fancy lady names.

They shared a game while they watched. Now and then, his mother would cup her hands over his eyes to block the view of the television set. Never at the scariest moment, usually while something dull was happening. She would gasp loudly, as if the most horrible thing had happened, though, and Owen would laugh.

He stayed up late on weekends because as soon as he went to bed she would start crying. And as he grew older, he began to wonder if his mother hated men. He never mentioned how handsome he thought Colin Clive was, or his troubling daydreams sparked by a sweaty Oliver Reed in *Curse of the Werewolf.* He watched how she half-smiled when the monsters caught the pretty girls.

As an adult, it seemed easier simply not to even attempt dating. He told himself it would only end in disaster. He didn't know the rules of the game, what even to say. He watched one of his co-workers sit on the edge of the receptionist's desk and felt more bewilderment than envy. He avoided all offers to get a drink after work and never attended the annual holiday party.

Spreadsheets gave the day structure. Being an accountant, a proper upstanding one, meant no cheating, no lies. Dinners with his mother helped with the nights, fending off loneliness. At first, after he'd earned his CPA and moved into a nearby efficiency apartment, Owen walked home every Monday and Friday night. Then, after his parents' divorce became final, he added Wednesdays. She never understood how to work the VCR he bought her. When she began forgetting things, such as paying bills or leaving on the oven, he did not hesitate to move back in with her. His old room felt small, but he wore it more like armor than a straightjacket.

Her last year, before the pneumonia took her, was spent at a nursing home. He came over every night after work to eat dinner with her. No sofa, just a mattress surrounded by stainless-steel safety bars. Like a crib for an adult. Her skin had faded to parchment and her fingers were all knuckles clenched around a cotton blanket.

"I want to go home," she would say. But the childhood home she wanted was a small house bulldozed decades ago in upstate New York. He would help feed her while the videotape played Bela Lugosi. "The Count," she murmured around a spoonful of soup that lacked any odor.

"I never drink..." he'd say. His mother answered "Wine," with more strength than she mustered for anything else. He'd kiss her cheek. "I'm gay, Mom," he'd say next. Or "I'm like a three-dollar bill" or once "I could marry in Massachusetts now." It should have been a relief to tell her, but she never reacted, never seemed to remember, and so it was simply one more standard action of his nightly visits like kissing the top of her head, which seemed to have a cradle cap where the hair thinned.

After the funeral, the house seemed far too still. He read about something called Gay Bingo. He knew the rules to bingo. But he never made it to the bar hosting the event. Along the way, he passed a pair of young men walking hand-in-hand. They reminded him of the boys in contemporary horror films, always more gorgeous than the damsels in distress. They looked like dolls.

The left doll stopped and sneered at him, lifting up the right's hand, fingers still interlocked, and kissed the back. The right doll snickered and Owen blushed.

"Bet this guy would like a show. He's practically drooling."

"Oh, sorry—" Owen began.

"Ugh, why do they let the trolls loose at night?" The left doll rolled his eyes and tugged the other down the street.

Owen's face burned. Wanting nothing more than to be out of sight and back at home, he looked around for a cab. Trolls were monsters that lived under bridges and had a liking for mutton. Trolls couldn't be accountants, couldn't work the number pad of the keyboard with their jagged claws.

Cars passed him by and he headed back to the corner with the subway station. He glanced back over his shoulder now and then. The steps to the station, dingy and wet and reeking of fresh urine, both promised retreat and reminded him that underground was where the trolls hid away from the rest of the world.

He felt guilty for calling in sick the following Monday but he could not bring himself to leave bed except to make his melted sandwich. When he took a bite, the tuna was sour on his tongue.

On his fortieth birthday Owen decided to end his life. His cousins had thrown him a party. He did not recognize most of the faces and the fact that so many strangers wanted to hug him or kiss him or slap his back left him shaking, and too nauseated to do more than pick at his ice cream cake, with its troubling layers of vanilla *then* chocolate and minty crème, utterly out of proper order.

Owen left their large condo clutching an armful of cards with gift certificates to stores he had never heard of. The moment he'd blown out the garish pink and white wax 4 and 0 candles, Owen knew the future. A life spent alone in his mother's house, a silent phone, a twin bed in which he'd die and not be found for days.

He stopped at the first sewer grate he came to and dropped the cards through the slots into darkness. They made a soft splash into whatever water flowed beneath. The sound, the image, reminded him of stories his mother would tease him with whenever they passed by a sewer. Gigantic albino alligators. She'd also told him that water towers imprisoned immense squid.

He wished one of those alligators—aligrators he had called them as a child—would burst through a manhole and crunch his old bones. There was never a monster around when you wanted. The thought stayed with him.

He didn't walk back to his apartment. Instead, he wandered until he came upon the old public library he'd visited in grade school. He missed the card catalog. He asked the librarian for help finding monsters. The books she found him reminded Owen of his mother's sofa, with their plastic dust jackets. But they were filled with photos of Frankenstein's Monster or Jack Pierce's other masterpieces. Creatures of greasepaint and celluloid. He needed real fangs.

Working the computer terminal, he found his quarry in 398. Folklore. He pulled out his pocket notebook in which he kept track of his daily, weekly, and monthly expenses, and tore off the first few pages. He wrote down the names and locales of the most promising creatures. Exotic names like *chupacabra* and *jentilak* filled him with excitement. He renewed his membership and checked out a stack of books.

The next day, bleary-eyed from too little sleep after a night of feverish reading, Owen went to work to type out his resignation. He sent it in via email after making the travel arrangements.

—

"Monsters?"

Owen nodded and tapped the book by his plate. "Old stories tell that a hag lives in a cave on the mountain. She has two mouths," he said and clicked his own jaws. "The second is hidden in her hair. She lures lost travelers and devours them."

Saul chuckled. "I would have guessed you were a businessman. Not a Van Helsing."

That distracted Owen for a moment; he would have liked to have been a Cushing Van Helsing more than a Van Sloan Van Helsing but doubted he had either's character.

"So what monsters have you slain?"

"None. I've searched everywhere. England. Scotland and Russia—"

"Where in Russia? I spent six months all over Perm Krai. I camped in the Urals."

Owen had never known anyone who had lived out of a tent for six days let alone months. Such a life, unfettered with a numerical address or zip code, seemed terrifying.

"You're really a professor, right? Studying folklore? I heard this part of Japan has some interesting history."

"I look like a professor?" Owen looked down at himself. His sports coat had seen better days. He imagined tweed patched at the elbows and smiled.

Saul shrugged. He stuffed rice into his mouth. Owen watched his Adam's apple bob with each swallow. Saul had a scrawny neck and several dark hairs peeked out of the collar of his t-shirt. Owen wondered how they would feel. Wiry or soft?

"I taught statistics at Princeton." Owen amazed himself with the lie.

Saul devoured his slices of pickle and Owen offered him the remaining pieces from his own plate. "And you're here because of this—"

"The Yama-uba."

Saul laughed. "I think that's what Japanese kids call grunge chic."

"The stories don't say what she wears." Owen looked at the faded cloth cover of the book.

"So you believe she exists?"

"The law of averages. I've looked for monsters everywhere. One of them has to be real."

Saul reached over the table and took hold of Owen's jacket lapel. He lifted it aside. "Are you packing silver bullets?"

Owen tried to hide his blush with an extra long sip of tea.

"Well, good luck with your hunt." Saul wiped his mouth then left a rumpled napkin in the center of his plate. "Maybe I'll see you later. If you need an assistant who knows almost nothing about the countryside."

Owen took too long to answer. Saul had left. Owen didn't know how to tell that, just once, he wished to be the one hunted.

—

At Nabekura, Owen avoided the paved road leading up the mountainside. It seemed likely that monsters had an aversion to macadam and steel and glass. He imagined the Industrial Revolution stranded them like polar bears in the shrinking Arctic. The Yama-uba might not have fed in decades. She might have withered away to bones frosted with the region's famous white dew.

He flipped through the pages of the library book. They were so brittle with age that corners cracked and fell like eggshell. He didn't seem able to focus on the words. If the Yama-uba proved to be another hoax, he didn't know what he'd do next. He couldn't conceive of a day after. The thought of being alive tomorrow filled him with dread.

He reached into his jacket pocket for a snack and remembered Saul's hand slipping past his lapel. Had that been a flirtation?

Owen clutched the packet of Cool Fran Lemon Biscuit Sticks. He marveled at their sweet smell, sweeter than any lemon ought to be; if he had never come to Japan to die, he would have never discovered so many treats. Though the chocolate he had purchased in Andreapol had been wondrous too. The Brosno dragon never rose from the lake but Owen had enjoyed the mild weather and the Babaevsky bars.

The beech trees on the mountain wore a golden-bronze raiment and whispered in a breeze that grew as the sun lowered to the horizon.

Owen moved higher. He rewarded exertion every so often with another biscuit. They crunched beneath his jaws. *Like tiny bones. I'm a troll snacking on bones*, he thought.

"Most people take the road."

He turned around. A Japanese girl stood in the shade. Long black bangs concealed her eyes. She wore layers and layers of clothing. Owen counted two stringy scarves, an overcoat with pale fur trim, strata of stockings with holes and socks showing beneath. Her *zori* crushed fallen leaves with their wooden soles.

"Scared you?" She stepped closer. Old-style headphones, the kind sold with old reel-to-reel players, lay atop the scarves around her neck.

"Startled would be more correct."

The girl, who might have been fourteen, fifteen, tapped her chin. "Don't litter."

"I won't." Guilty, he made a show of crumpling the empty package and putting it into his pocket.

"Good. The *kami* wouldn't like it."

"*Kami*?" The word sounded familiar.

She looked up the mountain a moment. "Spirits. If you believe in that sort of thing."

"I'm looking for one of them. The Yama-uba."

She giggled and repeated the name.

Owen's cheeks flushed and he felt foolish, as if he had stopped and asked her for directions.

"Why her?" she asked.

Owen shook his head and started hiking. The girl called out her question again. He answered without turning around. "Most people don't like being mocked."

"You're too late. She's gone."

He stopped and slid back a little. "Gone?" He muttered the word at first. "Gone?" He heard the girl climbing after him.

"Yes."

"As in dead?" He imagined a heap of bones forgotten on the mountainside.

The girl's eyes widened for a moment and she seemed ready to break into another bout of laughter. "No, no, no. She went to the city. Moriokashi. Or maybe Tokyo. It doesn't matter."

"How—"

"You really do want to find her." The idea seemed to perplex her and she stuck the frayed end of one scarf into the corner of her mouth. Her tongue was very pink.

"You're not some director, are you? She's not like those *yūrei* in J-horror. I hate those."

"But you've seen her…" Owen didn't know whether he should be thrilled to have finally found a monster to be real or disappointed that he'd arrived too late.

"She raised me. I ran away years ago." The girl pointed up the mountain. "Her cave is not far from here."

"I came all the way from Jersey," Owen said. He felt about to topple, as if his left foot wanted to take another step while the right wanted to turn back.

"Did she eat someone you know?"

"Not quite." Owen took out his notebook. He didn't know whether to cross out the last entry or not.

The girl must have turned on an mp3 player in her pocket because he heard noise coming from her headphones. He didn't care for popular music and couldn't understand why anyone would enjoy something that sounded like eerie whispers and smacking lips. "I could show you the cave. *Her* cave."

He shook his head. What would be the point?

She looked hurt and nibbled more at her scarf. Watching her do so threatened Owen's gag reflex. He imagined the girl living in a hole in the ground, gnawed bones shoved off to the side, kanji scratched on the walls. No wonder she dressed and acted so peculiar. "Why stay? I mean, if she's gone you're free to leave."

"Where would I go? I know the smell of the stone when it rains and the feel of the dirt at my back. When I'm there I can close my eyes and still see everything." Her response sounded petulant. "Every time I step out, there's this tiny voice, echoing my own. It tells me to go back. It's safe and solid, sleeping in the earth. Like my hair and fingers become roots sinking into the ground."

The way she talked about the cave made Owen's chest tighten. "Sometimes being safe is stifling." But after he said it, he remembered that his quest had failed. He'd have to return to America, to Trenton and his mother's house and retreat to his bedroom. He heard himself wheezing, trying to breathe.

He waited for the girl to walk away. But she didn't. They both stood there in awkward silence for a while.

"In all the books I've read about monsters, the authors always mention how man is afraid of the unknown. They even capitalize it. The Unknown. But they're wrong. I'm more afraid of what I expect, what I know I'll be doing tomorrow and the next day." He licked his lips. "And the next. I'd rather have a bit of the Unknown, anything but the Given."

The girl chewed her scarf harder for a moment. "Would you help me carry some things I want from the cave?"

He nodded and moved slowly to follow her.

He stopped when the brush rustled off to his right. A strong breeze? He couldn't be sure. Perhaps a squirrel, if they had them in Japan. He stopped to peer through the beech trees.

The girl called down to him but he remained there. She tramped back down to where he stood. Her music had grown louder.

"Thought I saw a *kami,*" he said with a grin.

Her face turned pale like milk. He almost laughed at how scared she looked. The dreary tune quieted for a couple of seconds, as if it had skipped a beat.

When she turned her head to look where he had, Owen took a step behind her. She was no taller than his chest. He couldn't resist teasing her as his mother had done to him. "You're not looking the right way." He brought his hands to her face, covering her eyes, while he smiled. Then he glanced down at the top of her head.

There was no mp3, no radio, making the hungry whispers. In her scalp a pair of leathery lips split and showed teeth sharper, more numerous, than a shark's. Fetid breath blew up and spittle slicked the surrounding hair.

Both Owen and the girl stayed motionless.

Owen felt cold, exposed, as if the temperature had suddenly dropped to freezing. Why couldn't he see his breath? Or hers, rising from between his fingers and rising from her scalp into his eyes. The fear that filled him made all his past anxieties seem like laughter. He could feel the muscles and tendons, nerves and bones within his hands, his entire body, recoiling, seeking to push away from the girl, this thing's body. But his hands refused to move.

He bit back the scream. Thoughts of dying sweated out of his every pore.

He clamped his hands tighter around her head. She said something in Japanese but his palm muffled her lower mouth. Then he twisted, hard, to the right. The snap sounded like stepping on a branch. The Yama-uba went limp against him. A soft sigh escaped her lips.

Owen let her fall to the ground. His hands trembled. He hugged them in his armpits. His teeth chattered.

The exposed skin of the Yama-uba's hands and neck grew loose, like dripping wax, then congealed in wrinkled folds. The nails long and yellowed and split. But her face, from smooth brow to rounded cheek and slight chin, her face remained a young girl's.

In movies, the monsters always looked different when they died, even poor Lawrence Talbot. He turned away from the body. He could not stand the sight of her face, serene despite the open stare.

He stumbled down the mountainside. Sometimes he fell and slid, ripping and staining his clothes. He almost collapsed when he saw the dark ribbon of the roadway. He sat down by the side of the road and put his head between his knees.

He wasn't sure how much time had passed when someone tapped him on the shoulder. He hesitated to look up, knowing, somehow, that he would see the Yama-uba's youthful face. But the thick mustached man who stood over him and spoke a rush of German looked concerned. Owen offered a weak smile that satisfied whatever Samaritan instinct the tourist possessed.

Owen stood up. When he brushed himself off, he felt the slight bulge of his notebook in a pocket. He slipped it out and turned to the final entry. He became annoyed when he thought he'd lost his pen, and then saw it by his feet. A sense of accomplishment filled him as he crossed out *Yama-uba*. No monsters after Y.

Then a cold draft of air brought a thought. Yeti. For a moment, Owen envisioned himself covered in thick furs and climbing snow-covered cliffs. A handsome Sherpa showed him tracks before suggesting they rest for the night. Sharing a tent, of course, to keep warm.

Sharing a tent with someone like Saul.

He almost wrote it down. Instead he scribbled in the word *Troll*, then crossed it out with a grin and headed back to town. He left the notebook behind.

Dragon Logic

Yoon Ha Lee

ONCE IN A REALM OF islands and morning mist, an emperor's son died. Perhaps he was murdered by a retainer. Perhaps he ran afoul of a vengeful spirit, or went hunting for tigers in a foreign land, or pined after a lady whose voice burned him with its beauty. There are many ways for princes to perish.

We are not much concerned with the prince. But the empress, oh the empress, she did not weep. They said her face was fair as foam, and that her hair rippled to her feet. She wore the colors of the sky and the colors of the sea, even after the prince's death, for the white of mourning is a color shared by sky and sea. But her sleeves were dry.

All the empire wept for the loss of this prince, yet in one woman's heart there was drought.

That is the beginning of the story they tell in the empire.

In the same realm, a monk who was not a monk studied a tablet left at a mountain shrine. The shrine was a small one, which saw few visitors. The monk who was not a monk would frown over this tablet's puzzle: circles inscribed within circles, triangles inscribed within triangles, lengths and areas to be computed. The tablet's mysteries yielded themselves piece by piece under the monk's devout studies.

One day the monk found the tablet gone. In its place was another with no puzzle for the mind's unraveling, only scratches meandering like the course of a river, cuts like the bite of a sword. The monk looked up and saw a man with noble features and strangely gloved hands.

The monk said, "You are not a man."

The man said, "That's all very well. You're not a monk."

Both of them were correct. The monk said, "Why do you linger here? Surely my devotions can bring you little hope of enlightenment." For the monk, who spoke rarely with other people, was really a woman.

"I am not interested in virtue," said the man, "but in the riddles you tangle and untangle."

"Go away," said the monk, "and find yourself someone who can recite the Lotus Sutra for the purification of your soul." The monk knew it by heart, of course, for all the good it did her.

The man ignored her. "I like your thoughts," he said. "They taste clean and clear and precise. They taste like angles and half-circles and straight lines." For the man was a dragon, a creature of storm winds and deep wells. He was bound to be intrigued by orderly things.

The monk said, "Is that why the shrine's tablet is gone?"

The man looked faintly embarrassed. "That's why I brought the shrine another one."

The monk sighed. The dragon's tablet bore little resemblance to the one it replaced. Already she missed its geometrical elegance and subtle numerical challenges. She couldn't blame him, though. If she sought in numbers the transcendence that was denied her by virtue of her birth, she supposed a dragon could yearn toward the same, however clumsily. "Let us look at it, then," the monk said.

The man's face brightened, like water beneath the moon.

This is the beginning of the story that matters.

The empress was of noble birth. Even after her elevation to the emperor's side, no one found had found any cause for reproach in her. She kept her face covered and took no lovers. She bore the emperor a fine heir. It was not her fault that the prince found himself an end earlier than his father's.

After years of doing everything that the emperor and his court expected of her, it is not surprising that the empress could no longer summon up the response they wanted, despite her grief.

The monk came to look forward to the dragon's visits, which occurred most often in the morning, before the mist burned away. The man brought a new tablet each time, taking away the last. She held each tablet—wood, usually, but sometimes ivory or stone—and ran her hands over the carved lines. Dragon curves, she called them.

One day, she said to the man, "You carve each curve with a single motion, without lifting—ah—hand from wood."

"Yes," said the man.

"They are beautiful curves," she said. And so they were, like the man himself. "Why do you claw through them?"

The man only looked at her sidelong. "There is a puzzle," he said, "but I do not know its answer."

Thoughtfully, the monk traced a looping curve of her own in the dirt. She realized as she did so that it could not be a dragon curve. She glanced at the man, whose eyes were the color of pond water.

In answer, he passed his hand over the curve on the ground. Three deep claw marks cut through it vertically. One of the claw marks passed through the loop twice, top and bottom. Both claw mark and curve began to fill with water.

The monk considered the water. "So that is the pattern," she said. This time she drew a circle, then a vertical slash through it. "This is not a dragon curve, because if you claw through its center, you will meet the circle twice. A true dragon curve can only be met once, no matter where you claw it." The monk would never have thought about such things on her own; to her the circle was the simplest and most pleasing of shapes, where all things began. She said as much to the man.

"You are a very strange monk," said the man. She knew by now that he meant it as a compliment.

The monk trailed a hand in the water, then tasted a drop. It was clear and sweet, and not a little wild, like the first rains of spring. "Why are your curves important?" she asked. She did not mean importance in the way of wars and grand intrigues. Rather, she wondered as to the focus of the dragon's peculiar devotions.

"I don't know," said the man. "I find shapes in the storm. I don't understand what they mean, and I am not a creature of patterns."

"We will figure it out," said the monk.

She was not wrong.

The emperor's court began to whisper unkind things about the empress. Her heart must be made of stone, they said, for her to remain unmoved by her own son's death—as if tears were the only way to mourn. The emperor approached her and asked her why she did not weep.

The empress bent her head. Her voice trembled as she answered from behind the silk screens. But the tears, the tears would not come.

The emperor could not endure her dry eyes. There had to be a way, he said, to bring tears to the empress's eyes so she might mourn properly.

One of his courtiers spoke to him of a monk at a small shrine. This monk, he said, was often visited by a dragon. And dragons bring rain.

Dragons are not very good at disguising themselves.

The monk was pondering the man's latest offering when the emperor's messenger arrived. This tablet was a new thing altogether. The monk could compute the areas of circles and triangles and rectangles, and other strange shapes formed by their boundaries. But this was a dragon curve, a whimsical thing undulating above a straight line. The man had clawed beneath the curve, dividing up the line. The monk lifted her head and gazed at the clouds. Of course. Rectangles. Divide the region between dragon curve and line into rectangles and find the area thus. However, the monk was dissatisfied, for the result would be inexact.

The messenger coughed politely and waited for the monk to look at him. The monk did. The messenger told the monk, "It will be trouble in the eyes of earth and heaven if the empress cannot weep."

The monk acknowledged the truth of this. All things had their proper order, and on earth it began with the emperor and his court. A woman's dry eyes might become drought in the rice fields.

The messenger said, "You must command your friend the dragon to bring water to the empress's eyes, or you will be exiled."

"You may tell the emperor that I understand," said the monk.

We do not know whether the messenger noticed that the monk was not a monk.

The next morning, the man came through the mist to find the monk tracing circles in the dirt, like eyes. "What's wrong?" he asked. "I didn't mean the tablet to distress you." Indeed, he seemed distressed at the possibility himself.

"It is not the tablet," the monk said. She explained the situation.

The man was silent for a moment. Then he said, "All water has its own path through the world, and the dragon king decrees these paths. He must have decided to withhold tears from the empress."

The monk said, "I will miss our mornings together. But I have two feet and they will take me into exile as the emperor commands."

"No," the man said. "The dragon king may govern the gates of water great and small, but this one gate I can open for your sake. The dragon king will kill me for my insolence. You must find my corpse and bury it, and build a shrine over it." He pulled off his gloves and offered them to her.

She took them. "How will I know where to find your corpse?" They both looked at the tablet with its whimsical dragon curve. "A river," the monk said, understanding.

"We are all trapped by the order of things," said the man, "empress or woman or dragon. It is time we found another way."

"By dying?" asked the monk. She reminded him that she could not pray for his enlightenment.

"You will find a way," said the dragon. He would not be moved.

Then they spoke of circles and triangles, of claw marks and the shapes of snow, and nothing more of farewell.

The man went to the emperor's palace, where everyone still wore white. The stories do not say if the man did the same. But he made his way to the empress amid her ladies in waiting.

"I know why you are here," the empress said, for she recognized the man for what he was.

"Do you?" asked the man. "Weep, or do not weep; it is your choice. That is what these others have taken from you. Mine is the way of water, if you would have it." And he held out his hand, his ungloved hand.

The empress was not unwise in the ways of the heavens. She knew something of what the man's fate would be. But she knew what was expected of her. She rested her hand in his.

Every gate in the palace slammed open, and the doors as well, like the roaring of thunder.

At last the empress wept, covering her face with her sleeves. The court was satisfied. But she never told anyone that her grief was no longer for the prince, but for the dragon and the monk for whom the dragon made his sacrifice.

Crops abounded in the years that followed.

The monk was not exiled. Instead, she walked the countryside until she found a river whose bends matched those of the dragon curve. Sure enough, there she found the man's body, rent by lethal claws. The man would never have used his own claws to such purpose, but the dragon king was another matter.

The monk gathered up the dragon's body and buried it, as he had instructed. There she built a shrine. At night she listened to the sound of the river, and in the morning sometimes she thought she heard the man's voice.

The monk had brought the man's last tablet with her, of course. She drew shapes in the dirt and scored them with rectangles, dividing and dividing each curve into pieces, but the answers never satisfied her.

One night as the moon rose high and pale and wild, she woke, thinking, Of course. She could divide and divide each dragon curve into *infinitely many* rectangles—and then the answer would be precise. She could put something together by taking it apart.

It would not have been possible with her hands, even dragon-gloved hands, but her devotions had taught her that the mind is capable of such wonders.

"Are you there?" she asked the man. For she knew it had never troubled the man that her meditations came from someone other than a man, someone who was not a proper monk.

We don't know what the river answered, and no one ever saw the monk after that. But later, when other people discovered the shrine, they were astonished by the many devotional tablets, carved by claw and smoothed by hand. We may guess that the monk and the man knew, by then, what mattered and what didn't—in their eyes, if not the eyes of the world.

And that is the end of the story that matters.

Born in the Pacific Northwest in 1979, **CATHERYNNE M. VALENTE** is the author of *Palimpsest* and the *Orphan's Tales* series, as well as *The Labyrinth, Yume no Hon: The Book of Dreams, The Grass-Cutting Sword,* and five books of poetry. She is the winner of the Tiptree Award, the Mythopoeic Award, the Rhysling Award, and the Million Writers Award. She has been nominated nine times for the Pushcart Prize, shortlisted for the Spectrum Award was a World Fantasy Award finalist in 2007. She currently lives on an island off the coast of Maine with her partner and two dogs.

K. BIRD LINCOLN spent 4 years in Japan precariously perched on a bicycle with 2 girls under the age of 5. Now she resides in Portland, Oregon and guiltily drives a car. Her other work has been published hither and thither in places such as *Strange Horizons, Ideomancer,* and *Flytrap*. She can be bribed with chocolate, espresso, or a good paranormal romance. For free fiction and more, check out geocities.com/kblincoln/mossyglen.html.

EKATERINA SEDIA resides in the Pinelands of New Jersey. Her critically acclaimed novels, *The Secret History of Moscow* and *The Alchemy of Stone* released from Prime Books. Her next one, *The House of Discarded Dreams*, is scheduled for 2010. Her short stories have sold to *Analog, Baen's Universe, Dark Wisdom* and *Clarkesworld,* as well as *Haunted Legends* and *Magic in the Mirrorstone* anthologies. Visit her at ekaterinasedia.com.

ERZEBET YELLOWBOY is the fiction editor of *Cabinet des Fées,* a fairy tale journal, and co-editor (with Sean Wallace) of *Jabberwocky Magazine*. She is also the founder of Papaveria Press, a private press specializing in handbound limited editions of mythic poetry and prose. Her stories and poems have appeared in *Fantasy Magazine, Goblin Fruit, Mythic Delirium, Electric Velocipede* and others and her second novel, *Sleeping Helena,* is due out next year. Visit her website at erzebet.com for more.

ROBERT JOSEPH LEVY is an author of books, stories and plays whose work has been seen Off-Broadway. He studied at Oberlin before graduating from Harvard and earning a Master of Arts degree in forensic psychology at John Jay College of Criminal Justice (CUNY). He lives with his husband and son in Brooklyn, NY.

A Clarion Workshop graduate, Robert has published three books with Simon & Schuster, including *The Suicide King* and *Go Ask Malice* (both set in the Buffy the Vampire Slayer universe), as well as another written pseudonymously that was named one of The New York Public Library's Best Books for the Teen Age 2008.

Robert would like to extend his appreciation to the generous and kind Christopher Barzak for providing the story's kanji.

RICHARD PARKS lives in Mississippi with his wife and a varying number of cats. He collects Japanese woodblock prints but otherwise has no hobbies since he discovered that they all require time. His fiction has appeared in *Asimov's SF, Realms of Fantasy, Lady Churchill's Rosebud Wristlet, Fantasy Magazine, Weird Tales,* and numerous anthologies, including *Year's Best Fantasy* and *Fantasy: The Best of the Year*. His third story collection, *On the Banks of the River of Heaven,* is due out in 2010 from Prime Books.

EUGIE FOSTER calls home a mildly haunted, fey-infested house in metro Atlanta that she shares with her husband, Matthew, and her pet skunk, Hobkin. Her publication credits number over 100 and include stories in *Realms of Fantasy, Interzone, Cricket, Fantasy Magazine, Orson Scott Card's InterGalactic Medicine Show, Baen's Universe*, and anthologies *Best New Fantasy, Heroes in Training, Best New Romantic Fantasy* 2, and *So Fey*. Her short story collection, *Returning My Sister's Face: And Other Far Eastern Tales of Whimsy and Malice*, is now available from Norilana Books. Visit her online at EugieFoster.com.

JAY LAKE lives in Portland, Oregon, where he works on numerous writing and editing projects. His 2009 novels are *Green* from Tor Books, *Madness of Flowers* from Night Shade Books, and *Death of a Starship* from MonkeyBrain Books. His short fiction appears regularly in literary and genre markets worldwide. Jay is a winner of the John W. Campbell Award for Best New Writer, and a multiple nominee for the Hugo and World Fantasy Awards.

KEN SCHOLES'S quirky, speculative short fiction has been showing up over the last eight years in publications like *Clarkesworld, Realms of Fantasy, Weird Tales* and *Writers of the Future Volume XXI.* Ken's first novel, *Lamentation*, debuted from Tor in February 2009. It is the first of five volumes in the *Psalms of Isaak* series. The second, *Canticle*, is in production for an October 2009 publication. Ken's first short story collection, *Long Walks, Last Flights and Other Strange Journeys*, is available from Fairwood Press. Ken lives near Portland, Oregon, with his amazing wonder-wife Jen West Scholes. He invites folks to look him up through his website.

JENN REESE is the author of *Jade Tiger*, a kung fu action-adventure romance (with tigers) from Juno Books. She currently lives in Los Angeles where she writes for a children's TV show, studies martial arts, and dreams of rain. You can follow her adventures at jennreese.com.

LISA MANTCHEV grew up in the small Northern California town of Ukiah and can pinpoint her first forays into fiction to the short stories she thumped out on an ancient typewriter. She makes her home on the Olympic Peninsula of Washington state with her husband Angel, her daughter Amélie and four hairy miscreant dogs. A list of her short fiction can be found on her authorly website (lisamantchev.com) and *Eyes Like Stars*, her debut novel, is due out Summer of 2009 from Feiwel & Friends. You can read more about it at theatre-illuminata.com.

STEVE BERMAN specializes in gay-themed tales of speculative fiction. He's traveled as far as Mongolia. He has edited such anthologies as *So Fey* and the annual *Wilde Stories*. His young adult novel, *Vintage, A Ghost Story*, was a finalist for the Andre Norton Award. For more of his stories, page through *Trysts* and *Second Thoughts*, his two short story collections.

YOON HA LEE'S fiction has appeared in *The Magazine of Fantasy and Science Fiction*, *Lady Churchill's Rosebud Wristlet*, and *Sybil's Garage*. She lives in Pasadena, CA with her husband and daughter.

ABOUT THE EDITOR

SEAN WALLACE is the founder and editor for Prime Books, which won a World Fantasy Award in 2006. In his spare time he is also co-editor of *Clarkesworld Magazine* and *Fantasy Magazine*; the editor of the following anthologies: *Best New Fantasy, Horror: The Best of the Year, Jabberwocky, Japanese Dreams,* and *The New Gothic;* and co-editor of *Bandersnatch, Fantasy, Phantom,* and *Weird Tales: The 21st Century.* He currently and happily resides in Rockville , MD , with his wife and two cats.

LaVergne, TN USA
01 December 2009
165584LV00001B/54/P